SLICE AND DICE

"Nothing," said the Blanchard. "Zip. No prints, no tracks; the ground's too hard and the grass too short. Because the gate was locked, the killer must have come over the wall."

"What could have done this?" Crimmins asked.

"Maybe a Florida panther migrating north because he's been squeezed out of his habitat. Or a wildcat spooked out of the Smokies, looking for new territory."

He emptied his glass. Southern Comfort.

"Or maybe some twisted maniac who's got himself a set of slice-and-dice fingers like Freddy Kruger. . . ."

THE WORLD OF DARKNESS

VAMPIRE
Dark Prince
Netherworld
Blood Relations
Blood on the Sun

WEREWOLF
Wyrm Wolf
Conspicuous Consumption
Hell-Storm
Watcher

MAGE
Such Pain
Mister Magick

WRAITH
Sins of the Fathers

Strange City (an anthology)

Published by HarperPrism

THE WORLD OF DARKNESS
Werewolf

Watcher

Based on
The Apocalypse

Charles Grant

HarperPrism
An Imprint of HarperPaperbacks

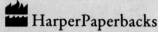
HarperPaperbacks
A Division of HarperCollins*Publishers*
10 East 53rd Street, New York, N.Y. 10022-5299

ISBN 0-06-105672-3

HarperPrism is an imprint of HarperPaperbacks.

First printing: June 1997

Printed in the United States of America

Visit HarperPaperbacks on the World Wide Web at
http://www.harpercollins.com/paperbacks

❖ 10 9 8 7 6 5 4 3 2 1

*For everyone at the real Chattacon, guests and organizers alike, for allowing me to do what I did to them here.
Even though I didn't ask.*

1

A werewolf moon hung over the valley, but there were still too many places for shadows to hide.

Branches creaked in the passing of a slow wind; a scrap of paper trembled in the gutter; a dog barked nervously, yipped, and fell silent; the blare of a distant freight train sounded dull, sounded hollow.

The single flap of night-black wings.

The not quite audible step of something large on dying grass.

October night, with a hint of frost and blood.

Polly Logan wasn't scared. She liked to walk through the middle of the night. She had friends, lots of friends, and they wouldn't let anything hurt her. The only thing was, they didn't like it when she left the house for a walk. Not after sunset, anyway. Certainly not alone.

But she wasn't scared.

The town of Lookout Mountain was too small to have bad people who would want to do bad things to someone like her. It was a pretty town. A nice town, high enough above the world that she could almost touch the sky. Not at all like Chattanooga, sprawled down there in the valley, at the base of Lookout Mountain itself. It was too big, that city; too many wide streets and too many dark streets, too many people moving around all at once. It made her nervous, and she didn't like to go there, not even to the doctor who took care of her and kept her well.

Except when they took her to the aquarium, that is. That part was fun, and she never got tired of it. You ride up to the top of a real long, shiny escalator, then walk down and around, down and around, with so many fish, so many colors, and the gentle sound of running water all around her all the time.

That was fun.

This was fun.

Walking along the street, listening to the night, watching the stars and the werewolf moon.

Not that she really believed in werewolves.

She knew she wasn't as smart as most people, but she also knew she wasn't a little girl anymore either. She was a big girl, nearly twenty-five, practically a woman, and big girls who were practically women didn't believe in werewolves and vampires and ghosts and big hairy monsters who lived in the bottom of the Tennessee River.

They just weren't so.

Just ahead, on the corner not far from her destination, a flock of autumn leaves swirled in the light sifting from the streetlamps. She watched the spinning colors, and giggled when they darted toward her suddenly. She used her hands to bat them away from her face, turning with them, giggling, until they all fell down.

"Fun," she whispered, and plucked a stray leaf from her long blond hair. It was perfect, not a rip in it, so she tucked it into her down parka, reminding herself to show it to Miss Doris in the morning.

After she had her visit with Kyle.

A blush touched her cheeks, and she swiped a finger across them as if to brush the blush away.

Kyle.

She shivered with pleasure, and quickened her step.

This was fun.

It didn't matter that all the houses she passed were either dark or only had a single light burning over the front door; it didn't matter that the only sounds she heard were her footsteps on the pavement, and the soft sigh of her breathing.

This was fun.

It was nearly Halloween, and it was fun.

She turned the corner, smiling broadly to herself, once in a while sweeping a hand over her face to push the hair away.

"You'll come to see me, won't you?" he had asked just that afternoon, smiling so hard his face squinched up, and all she could see were his lips and his freckles: "It's a pain being all alone, you know? Why don't you stop by, and I'll give you a private tour."

Too surprised and shy to speak aloud, she had nodded so hard she nearly made herself dizzy, and ran all the way back to the house, where she sat in her room and stared at all the pictures of the animals she had drawn, waiting for them to tell her what to do. To tell her it was okay.

A long time ago, Miss Doris had said, "Don't you ever speak to strange men, you hear me, child? They'll take advantage of you, poor thing, and you won't even know it. A strange man tries to speak to you, touch you, you come straight home and tell me right away, and I'll see to it he never speaks to young girls again."

Miss Doris said that a lot.

Polly always nodded, too, and swore she would never, ever let anyone she didn't know touch her or speak to her, unless Miss Doris said it was all right first. She may not be very smart, but like Miss Doris always said, she wasn't stupid either.

But Kyle, he was different. She didn't know why, exactly, but he was.

He worked at the little park where the town stopped at the end of the mountain, sometimes in the daytime and sometimes in the nighttime. He wore a uniform, just like Officer Zielke did, even though he wasn't a real policeman. He helped the tourist people who came from all over to look at the Civil War monument, or to look down at Chattanooga and take lots of pictures, or who wanted to know how many states they could see from the bluff on a real clear day.

He was kind. Really kind. And he never, ever tried to touch her. Never, ever made fun of her.

Not like the kids in her school. The one she went to before she came to live with Miss Doris, that is.

Polly, Polly,
Oh good Polly,
Ain't it true
You're off your trolley?

That wasn't fun.

That had made her cry.

Kyle didn't make her cry. He made her laugh. He made her cheeks feel all warm and her tummy all cozy. He once bought her an ice cream cone, and gave her his handkerchief when the cone started to melt all over her fingers.

Polly, won't you come and visit me tonight?

She ducked her head and hurried on, counting her footsteps, thinking about Kyle and how he lived in his very own castle and how she might live in a castle, too, one day. Why, she might even be called a—

"Polly Logan, my heavens, what on earth are you doing, young lady?"

She jumped, a hand darting to her throat to stop a scream, when a round, little man stepped out from behind a thick, tall hedge. He didn't have much hair, and what he did have was pure white. His coat was long, his hands gloved, and behind him on a leash was a tiny dog that looked all hair and legs.

"Oh, Mr. Abbott, you scared me!"

Baines Abbott grinned an apology. "I'm sorry, dear, but I didn't expect to see anyone out this late. Hush, Beau," he snapped at the dog, who hadn't done anything but growl a little. "Dog thinks he's a giant sometimes. Polly, does Miss Doris know you're out so late?"

"Yes, sir, she sure does." She nodded vigorously. "I'm just taking my . . . my evening constitutional."

He laughed silently. "Polly, you are truly something else, do you know that?" He looked quickly side to side and gave her a wink and a silly pretend scowl. "Okay, young lady, I won't tell. But only if you promise me you'll get yourself home right away, you hear? Little lady like you ought to be in bed this time of night." He squinted at the sky and tilted his head. "Besides, it looks like there's some weather coming." He sniffed. "Rain or snow, I can't tell."

She looked as well, and saw a silver-edged cloud cut the huge moon in half.

"Home, Polly," Mr. Abbott said gently. "Go home."

She nodded, promised him she'd just go around

the next corner, and head straight back for her bed, cross her heart and hope to die.

Beau barked, once.

Abbott hushed him, laughed, and walked away quickly, the terrier scampering to keep up.

Oh, my, Polly thought; oh, my.

Her heart slammed against her chest, her lungs worked double-time, and suddenly her knees didn't want to work anymore.

That big, old moon wasn't very pretty anymore.

Maybe Mr. Abbott was right. Maybe she ought to turn right around and go back home before Miss Doris found out she was gone. She would apologize to Kyle first thing tomorrow, and he would understand. He always understood. He certainly wouldn't be mad. He wouldn't want her caught out in a storm.

Polly, Polly.

Moonlight faded.

The wind kicked, and the leaves didn't tickle anymore.

She frowned in indecision as she looked over her shoulder, biting down softly on her lower lip. She only had one more corner to turn, though; just one more corner. She could run real fast, tell Kyle she had to go home, and run back, and nobody would ever know she'd been gone.

The short street was empty.

One car was parked at the curb, its windshield like a narrow, black eye.

All the houses were dark, not even a porch light, not even a glow from the handful of small shops.

Not even the lights of Chattanooga reflected in the sky.

Something had changed.

Now that Mr. Abbott and Beau had gone, the night was somehow different.

It was the same wind, and the same leaves dancing, and the same stars, and the same buildings there always were . . . but it was all different, too.

It wasn't nice anymore.

I'm not scared, she told herself.

Polly, Polly.

I am not scared.

She ran to the corner and looked down the street. Empty. Dark.

When the blacktop ended, the castle began, fieldstone and high, higher still with turrets on either side of Point Park's high arched entrance. It was dimly lighted, and the light stained the stone with shadows, making the black iron gate beneath the arch look solid. She didn't know why, until she realized all the lights in the small park beyond were out.

"Oh, dear," she whispered.

She didn't know what to do.

If Kyle was there, why were the lights out? If Kyle wasn't there, why hadn't he told her?

She walked closer, very slowly, biting softly on her lower lip.

This was kind of like that night last summer, when she had seen the pretty light in the sky. She really was scared then, because it was sun-bright and almost green, and it moved very fast over the mountain, too fast for her to follow. At first she thought that maybe she had imagined it, like Miss Doris tells her that she imagines lots of things. But it came back a few minutes later, and it was lower, and although she couldn't see what made it, she had a bad feeling. She had a bad feeling that whoever was in the thing that made the light was in big trouble.

Then it disappeared.

Just like that, it disappeared.

And just like that, before she could breathe again, there was a really bright light, this one all orange and blue and green and yellow, and a loud noise that nearly knocked her to the ground.

And then it was dark again.

And no one had believed her when she told them she'd seen a light.

Other people had seen it and told the television and the newspapers about it, too, but no one had believed her.

They hardly ever did.

Now they wouldn't believe her when she told them that the lights in the park were all out. They weren't supposed to be; Kyle was supposed to keep them on all the time.

Her eyes widened.

Maybe he's hurt.

She walked faster.

Maybe he fell down when the lights went out, and now maybe he's hurt.

She almost ran, a tear blinding one eye, the wind nudging her, leaves suddenly lunging out of the trees to tangle in her hair and scratch at her face.

She nearly collided with the gate, stopping herself just in time by grabbing the bars.

"Kyle?" Very quietly; she didn't want to get into trouble.

No answer.

"It's Polly." Very quietly; she didn't want to get caught.

There were no lights, but she could see the trees anyway from the oddly muted glow of the city hidden below. Dark holes in the night, and boulders and trees along the rim of the bluff.

"Kyle?"

She heard a noise: a snuffling, and a low growl.

Her mouth opened; she couldn't say his name again.

Then something reached through the bars and grabbed her ankle. She yelled, and fell onto her rump, kicking and screaming, until her ankle was free. Kicking again and crying until she saw the hand, its fingers curled and trembling hard.

"Polly."

Until she saw Kyle's face, pressed against the bars.

"Polly . . . please . . ."

It was red.

2

Sometimes, when he was alone, he liked to call himself Lon Chaney, the Man of a Thousand Faces.

Not that he had a thousand faces, or even a couple of dozen, for that matter. But it felt like it. A touch here, a mustache there, once in a while a hairpiece, and he was, as always, someone else.

It didn't take much. People seldom saw what they thought they did.

What he did have, however, was a thousand names.

For a while, back at the beginning, he had tried to keep track of them, just for the hell of it. He gave up after five years; the list had grown too long. Now he let the others do it, to make sure there were no duplications. He had enough trouble as it was keeping in mind the name he had now. A hazard of the game; like playing six roles in a play simultaneously, you have to make sure you react to all the right cues, or you'll be exposed for the fraud you are.

All of them.

"You know," he said to the man on the other end

of the line, "just once I'd like to be John Smith, you know what I mean? Or Harry Truman."

There was no response.

The man sighed and shook his head. It was a good thing he liked his job, because the people on the other end didn't have much of a sense of humor. Especially when it came to something like this.

"Mr. Blanchard," his caller said. A mild scolding, and a suggestion to get on with it.

Miles Blanchard rolled his eyes at the empty motel room, and picked up a tumbler from the scarred nightstand. The Southern Comfort—no ice, that would be a crime—tasted good. He made sure his caller heard him drinking.

"Mr. Blanchard."

"I know, Mr. Crimmins, I know, I know." Wearily he swung his legs onto the bed, toed off his shoes, and settled himself against the headboard.

The room was in twilight; the drapes were closed; the only light was from a lamp on a table beside the bolted-to-the-dresser television. No sounds in the corridor. No traffic outside save for the occasional arrival of a bus at the depot next door.

It was well after midnight.

"The girl's name is Polly Logan. She's a retard—"

"Mr. Blanchard!"

Blanchard ignored him. "—who's living with a woman named Doris Maurin. It's a foster care thing mixed in with a halfway house for loonies or something. The kid has no family. She can stay on her own if she has to—and apparently she will one of these days—but she's been in and out of institutions all her life what with one thing and another, but mostly because of the no family thing. She's only been out of this last one for fourteen months. The Maurin woman is supposed to get her used to the outside. Help her get a job to pay rent, stuff like that."

"Was she hurt?"

"Nope. A bruise on her ass when she fell, that's all. A couple of scrapes on her hands. Nobody knows why she was at the park in the first place. She's not talking to anyone. She just sits in her room and draws pictures of her favorite animals or something."

"Have you seen them? The pictures?"

"No, sir, I haven't."

"Do so, Mr. Blanchard."

"Sure thing."

The drapes fluttered as a draft slipped through the window frame, a touch of November that made the room seem darker, and smaller.

"Continue."

Blanchard shifted. "Apparently the Gellman guy tried to grab her leg or something when she got there, and that's what knocked her over. Scared her half to death. He was already mostly dead, and he was absolutely dead by the time the paramedics got there. A neighbor walking his dog called them when he heard the girl screaming."

"Who was this neighbor?"

"A guy named Baines Abbott. He runs a gift shop up on the mountain. Tourist stuff mostly. The Civil War, things like that."

"What does he know?"

"That Gellman's dead, that's all. He's a harmless old coot. For now."

"If you say so, Mr. Blanchard. Did this Gellman say anything to the girl?"

"Nope."

"Cause of death?"

"No blood." He grinned at the ceiling.

"Mr. Blanchard . . ."

"Yeah, yeah, right, I'm sorry." He took another drink and stared at the tips of his black socks. "Simply put, he bled to death from several deep gashes—one across the chest, one across the throat, a couple across the gut. He was attacked on a path just inside the entrance, according to the local M.E., and dropped pretty much right away. Evidently, he crawled to the gate, probably trying to get some help. Just bad luck the kid showed up when she did."

"I wouldn't call that bad luck, Mr. Blanchard."

"I meant for the kid."

"I see."

Blanchard grinned again, drank again. He had never met the man who called himself Terrence Crimmins, and frankly never wanted to. Twisting the guy's tail long-distance was one thing; face-to-face would be something else again. He had no illusions about the man's power, or the danger he represented. Blanchard was perfectly satisfied receiving his instructions, and his payments, via intermediaries or the mail. Or, on special occasions like this, over the phone.

Crimmins was the only man Miles Blanchard had ever feared.

He glanced at the black box that cradled the original receiver, at the quartet of tiny red bulbs that glowed steadily on the side, an indication that the scrambler was in charge and hadn't been breached.

"The police," Crimmins said calmly.

"Nothing. Zip. No prints anywhere, the ground's too hard and the grass too short. No weapon. No prints or anything else in the blood Gellman left behind on the blacktop. Because the gate was locked, they figure the killer had to have come over the wall that extends on either side of that castle thing in front, but they can't find out where. He sure as hell didn't climb up the bluff.

"As for the alleged assailant, it has been suggested to the papers that this could be a unique case, nothing more. A Florida panther migrating north because he's been squeezed out of his habitat. Or a wildcat spooked out of the Smokies, looking for new territory." He emptied his glass. "Or maybe some twisted maniac who's got himself a set of slice-and-dice fingers like Freddy Kruger."

"Kruger, Mr. Blanchard?"

Blanchard rolled his eyes again, wishing his employers would take a look at the real world once in a while. It would make his life a whole lot easier. "A guy in the movies, sir. Kind of a monster who has knives stuck to his fingers."

"I see."

I'll bet, Blanchard thought and yawned silently.

"And do they believe it?"

Blanchard nodded, glad Crimmins couldn't see how smug he looked. "Yes, sir, they sure do. Sort of." He glanced at a copy of the *Chattanooga Times* on the bed beside him. "The TV says it's a maniac. The papers say it's an animal. They have experts on both sides coming out of their ears."

"My congratulations, Mr. Blanchard. An interesting bit of confusion. Well done, indeed. How do you think they will resolve it?"

"My best guess? It's been eleven days, so probably they'll come down on the maniac theory. Gellman wasn't eaten, and there were no parts missing. Plus, barring any other sightings or attacks, it's probably going to die down to just some editorials by the weekend, back page by Monday. They've still got conventions coming down here, Thanksgiving tourists, things like that. I don't

think anyone wants to stir that particular pot
again."

"Ah." Nothing else for a moment until, "Please
wait."

Blanchard crossed his legs at the ankle and stared
at the ceiling. As always, from the sound of it, the
man was on a speaker phone, and right now he'd be
conferring with whoever else was in the room.
Wherever that was. Blanchard hated this part. The
waiting. He had long ago stopped trying to second-
guess his employer; he hadn't yet been right, and
once it had nearly gotten him killed. He only hoped
they wouldn't want him to take care of the kid. She
seemed really sweet, a real innocent. And from what
she had seen, and from what he had learned of her
reaction and current condition, she'd probably be
back in an institution anyway before the year was
out. Traumatized for life, or something like that.

"Mr. Blanchard?"

"Still here, sir."

"After you check on that poor child's drawings, we
would like you to stay down there for a few days
more. Say, at least until Thanksgiving weekend. Look
around. Keep the media . . . distant. Be aware."

Blanchard frowned. "Sir, no offense, but I don't
think that's a good idea. I've been down here for
nearly two weeks already. I've been all over that
damn mountain, and I haven't found a thing except
rocks and bushes. There just isn't anything there.
Besides, nobody's seen anything, nobody's heard
anything, nobody knows anything. The girl is a joke,
and Gellman's dead. If I keep snooping around without good cause, somebody's bound to get suspicious."

"Your . . . kit isn't reliable?"

He glanced at the compact makeup chest on the

dresser, and at the small drawers beneath it where the rest of his tools were. "I don't want to sound immodest, Mr. Crimmins, but you already know I'm pretty damn good at what I do. But I have to remind you, sir, that I'm not a miracle worker. This may not be . . . where you are, sir, but these people aren't stupid. I'd like to suggest that the last thing you want me to do is to have to leave town in a hurry."

A pause before: "I'll think about it. Be available tomorrow night."

The connection broke, and Blanchard immediately unhooked the scrambler, dropped the receiver onto its own cradle, and packed the scrambler in a small padded carrier he placed in a suitcase kept in the room's closet. He did this all without thinking. It wasn't until he had made sure the telephone was still working that he aimed a kick at the dresser.

"Son of a bitch!"

He snatched up the bottle of Southern Comfort from the floor beside the bed and nearly flung it against the wall, catching himself just in time.

Damn them, he thought, rage tightening his chest; why the hell don't they come down here for a while? Why don't they spend some time in this two-bit burg with nothing but college basketball games and a fucking fish house to kill time with? Why don't they stay in a place where the fucking bar closes at midnight?

Jesus H. on a—

The telephone rang.

"What?" he demanded, taking a pull straight from the bottle.

"Is this Miles Blanchard?"

A woman, her voice deep and husky, and he blinked several times before he realized who it was.

He swallowed quickly, nearly choking himself. "Yes, it sure is."

"This is Della speaking. We spoke earlier this evening? I tried to reach you before, Miles, but the phone was busy."

He sat on the edge of the bed, the bottle between his legs. "Sorry, darlin'. Unfortunately, business never stops in my line of work."

"This late?" Honey and velvet now. "My, my, you Northern boys don't rest at all."

He sighed heavily, loudly. "I know. It's a crime, but what are you going to do?"

"So . . . are you still up for some company?"

"Oh, yes. Now more than ever."

"Wonderful. I have to ask you a question, though, before I come over. Please don't take offense."

He waited.

"Are you a cop?"

He gaped at the receiver, grinned at his reflection in the long mirror over the dresser, and said, "Darlin', believe me, the last thing in the world I am is a cop."

And the first thing he did after hanging up was take his gun from the nightstand, slip it into its holster, and put it all into the bottom dresser drawer, beneath his white shirts.

The last thing he did was utter a quick prayer that he wouldn't have to kill this woman who called herself Della.

3

The autumn leaves were long gone, and the blue of
the sky over the Capitol had shifted from hazy summer soft to clear winter sharp. Shortly after sunset,
whitecaps rose and sprayed ahead of a strong wind
that gusted down the Potomac. Flags snapped like
gunshots, and automobiles trembled when they
were caught broadside at the city's wider intersections. Light from streetlamps and Christmas decorations in store windows, looked brittle and slightly
hazed.

The Mall was nearly deserted.

A few scraps of paper tumbled across the short,
browning grass, and a long, brown cat raced for the
leeward shelter of the Metro station.

A man, his hands burrowed in black topcoat pockets, watched the cat from the steps of the Air and
Space Museum, and smiled to himself as it briefly,
vigorously, attacked a candy wrapper that skittered
ahead of it, before sitting calmly, only its tail twitching.

It looked in his direction only once. And when it
did, he saw the eyes gleaming narrow, and sensed

the soft warning growl deep in its throat before it decided to take a moment to preen its whiskers.

He laughed without a sound and left the museum behind as he angled between parked cars and crossed the street, pausing on the opposite sidewalk while he checked his watch, for no reason at all.

Up to his left, the Capitol building seemed inordinately small despite all the spotlights, hunkered down against the cold black of the early-evening sky.

A siren called, somewhere to his right.

On the wind rose scents he ignored—gasoline and warm metal, cooling stone and exhaust, a young man hurrying east on the far side of the Mall, an old woman lying asleep, wrapped in rags and newsprint, dying.

He shivered when the night air slipped down his upraised collar, and he hunched his shoulders before moving on, watching his streetlight shadow slip ahead of him, and swing behind. He had no clear idea of where he wanted to go, or where he would end up; for the moment, just being outside, being able to breathe fresh air, was good enough.

The wind died.

He walked on, paying little attention to the traffic or the occasional pedestrian. He heard only the sound of his heels on the pavement, looked up only when he wanted to cross another street. He supposed he should head for home, but he knew he would be just as restless there, and more confined. He'd only end up going out again.

He rounded a corner into a small, upscale shopping district and had to sidestep around a sidewalk Santa Claus packing up his gear while talking to a little girl who kept giggling and glancing shyly up at her mother.

It was a scene straight out of Hollywood, and he couldn't help a grin as he glanced back in time to see the child and Santa solemnly shake hands. The handshake was a promise, and he hoped someone would keep it.

Fifteen minutes later he paused in front of a newsstand looking ready to close up for the day. A low bench beneath the window held picked-over stacks of out-of-town and foreign newspapers; in narrow racks that flanked the bench were magazines that were, in the main, concerned with news and opinion; the foreign ones here were mostly fashion and sports.

He didn't see anything to spark his interest.

All right, he told himself; this is getting ridiculous. Make up your mind.

His problem was not boredom, nor any particular malaise. It was a lovely evening, the decorations were cheerful, and aside from the persistent restlessness, his own mood was close to buoyant.

It was hard not to break into a run, just for the sheer joy of it.

The problem was an uncommon but not unfamiliar situation: at present he was involved in no active assignments, urgent or otherwise, and as far as he could tell from the reports he received, there didn't seem to be anything coming up anytime soon that would require his attention, peripheral or otherwise. Which left nothing but those same reports to be read, studied, and, the chances were, burned or shredded and summarily stashed in the circular file.

He had, at the same time, plenty to do and nothing to do at all.

He also knew that the holidays would soon take care of that. The lull before yet another storm.

The days between Thanksgiving and Christmas
were potentially explosive. Depression and psy-
choses tended to build during these few weeks as
daylight shortened, the cold deepened, and some
people were reminded by the season's excess of all
the things they didn't have, or believed they didn't
have—family, money, expensive gifts, connections
with others. By tomorrow, or the next day, or the day
after that, there would undoubtedly be a flurry of
kidnappings, murders, and suicides; then he would
have more work than he would have time to complete.

Reading. Studying. Looking for the clues that
would lead him to his prey.

It was out there; it always was.

He knew it; he just couldn't see it yet.

But that was tomorrow. Or the next day. Or the
day after that.

Right now, he was . . . monumentally bored.

He laughed at himself as he walked on, absently
pushing a long-fingered hand back through dark-
brown hair lightly flecked with silver and curling
slightly toward his shoulders. A block later he turned
into a residential side street whose lighting was
nearly nonexistent, most its illumination owed to
electric candles in townhouse windows and colored
lights around the doors. Brick and polished granite
facades, swept stoops and sidewalks, plus waist-
high, black iron fencing in front of each building,
attested to the modest affluence of those who lived
inside. Traffic was swift here as automobiles took
shortcuts from one thoroughfare to another.

An elderly couple passed him, arm in arm, shopping bags in their free hands, chatting softly to each
other in French.

He nodded to them and moved on, thinking that

maybe, before he completely exhausted himself, he would give it up, go home, get some sleep.

Tomorrow, remember, he told himself; or the next day, or the day after.

A soft, sudden cry cocked his head, and he glanced over his shoulder. The shopping bag couple stood with their backs to him and a narrow-bored tree, facing someone taller and much heavier, a kid, whose features were in shadow. He instantly stepped to one side, blending his own dark form with that of a curbside tree. It didn't take but a few seconds to understand that the kid posed a threat, and, by the way the old Frenchman slipped a protective arm around the woman's shoulders, a dangerous one as well.

A swift scan of the area showed him no signs of Metro police, nor were there any nearby pedestrians he could call on for assistance.

The kid leaned forward, a clear menace, and the couple cringed.

The man knew this wasn't his affair, but there was fear down that street, and very likely death if the kid was spooked or didn't get what he wanted; he wasted no more time.

He unbuttoned his coat, grabbed a cellular telephone from his pocket, and as he headed back down the sidewalk, put it to his ear. He spoke just loudly enough to be heard, while he gestured extravagantly and impatiently with his left arm. He was a man clearly absorbed in his conversation, the rest of the world nonexistent.

The kid stiffened as the man approached, turning his back slightly to the nearest townhouse, blocking easy view of whatever weapon he held.

"I don't care," the man in black snapped. "The senator wants it done tonight, so make sure that you do it. Screw up and it's your ass, not mine."

He could see the victims' eyes pleading, could see the Frenchman's mouth open, could see a shift in the kid's stance which immediately stifled any call for help the others might have made.

"Whatever you have to do," he demanded as he passed them, noting the way the potential assailant had his right hand tucked into his coat at chest level. "Just make the calls, all right? Just make the damn calls."

A single step past them, and in one swift motion, he jammed the phone into his coat pocket and pulled out a gun, turned, and placed the barrel hard against the kid's nape, to make sure he knew he wasn't bluffing.

"FBI," he said, the first thing that came to mind. "Drop it, get to your knees."

It always happened: that eternal split second when the target had to make a decision whether or not he had a chance of escape or retaliation. A subtle tension, a subtle shift of balance, sometimes a held breath—all the signs, and no infallible way of reading them.

The man pressed the barrel harder against the kid's neck, just a little and leaned closer, just close enough for the man to hear the deep guttural snarl.

"All right, man, all right," the kid said wearily, shoulders slumping in defeat. "Just take it easy, okay? No problem. Ain't gonna hurt nobody."

"Drop it," he insisted.

The right arm lowered slowly, and he saw the glint of a blade just before he heard it strike the pavement near the curb. "Down!" he ordered, as his right foot kicked the knife out of reach.

The kid slumped obediently to his knees and sat back on his heels, his hands already behind his back without having to be told.

The man in black wasted no time—as he bound the wrists with handcuffs, he asked the woman to knock on the nearest door and have someone call the police; she didn't need to be asked twice. Then he stopped the old man in the act of reaching for the blade. "The police will take care of it. You just relax, catch your breath."

Once the kid was secured, he had him sit against the trunk of the tree, legs splayed. He was young, thin, wearing nothing but a T-shirt under his coat. A sketch of a mustache darkened his upper lip.

"Thank you," the old man said.

He smiled. "My pleasure. Believe me."

"*Comment vous appellez-vous, monsieur?*"

"Turpin," said the man. "Richard Turpin."

The old man nodded to the weapon. "He would have killed us, I think."

The blade was long, two-edged, and by the gleam of it, freshly sharpened. It wasn't a stabbing knife; it was a slasher, meant to open arteries no matter how it was whipped at the intended victim.

"I didn't want to kill nobody," the kid grumbled behind a scowl.

"You will go to jail," the old man said.

"Fuck you," the kid said, rolling his eyes and shaking his head. "You got lucky, that's all. Fucking angel here, you oughta kiss his ass."

Without a word, Richard gestured to the old man—*wait for your wife by the steps*—and squatted in front of the still grumbling kid, surely, Richard thought, barely out of his teens. He stared until the kid met his gaze.

"You have a name?"

"What's it to you?"

"You have a name?"

The kid looked away in disgust. "Fuck off."

"Do you have a name?"

The kid sighed heavily and looked back. "Chris, okay? You got a problem with that?"

Richard smiled, barely. "Tough dude like you, you're called Chris?"

The kid sneered. "Dude? Dude? You some kinda joke, man?" He laughed and looked at the street. "Dude. Jesus Christ." He laughed again.

Richard leaned closer, his voice lower, his back to the old Frenchman. "Tell me something, Chris—do you want to live until morning?"

The kid rolled his eyes . . . and looked.

Richard knew exactly what he saw—an ordinary man somewhere in his thirties, lean, clean-shaven, with eyes that tucked up slightly at the corners; a hint, some thought, of the Orient there.

He also saw the face shimmer, saw the green that filled those eyes; not emerald, but green fire.

He saw the teeth.

It lasted no longer than a blink.

It was enough.

"Oh, man," the kid said hoarsely, pushing back as if he could force his way through the trunk to the other side. "Oh man, what the—"

Richard patted his cheek once, not lightly. "Be a good boy, Chris. Watch your mouth." A smile, a shimmer, a hint of teeth again, more like fangs. "And watch your back, son. Nights are long this time of year."

The kid couldn't speak; he could only gape as he tucked his legs in, huddling now, bravado evaporated.

With a deep breath Richard rose, and less than a minute later the first patrol car arrived with lights and sirens. He identified himself to the officer who jumped from the vehicle before it had completely stopped and filled him in on the incident.

And as soon as the inevitable confusion became acute enough, he slipped away; they wouldn't know he was gone until it was too late.

He didn't worry about anything the kid might say. In an hour the boy would convince himself he hadn't seen a thing, that it had all been lights and shadows. A shame about the old couple, though. They had fussed over him to an almost embarrassing degree, and he didn't have the heart to tell them he wasn't what they thought he was.

Not in their wildest dreams.

Not in their worst nightmares.

Once he was back on the street again, however, his step was lighter and his smile broad.

What he hadn't tried to explain, and what they might not fully comprehend, was that his momentary pleasure of helping them out of a dangerous, perhaps lethal, situation, came not entirely from the possibility of saving their lives. It was wonderful that no one had been hurt; it was a bonus that it had all happened so cleanly in less time than it would take them to tell it when they called family and friends.

But it was even better, and in some ways more important, that another member of the opposition would now be off the streets for a while.

That kid wasn't a drug lord, wasn't a mass murderer, wasn't a major thief wanted in a dozen states.

But as young as he was, he was the opposition.

Clumsy, maybe; maybe even inept.

But he was the opposition, even if he wasn't the usual prey.

Chalk one up for the good guys, he thought.

For a change.

In the words of her first hang-gliding instructor, Trish McCormick was "drop-dead gorgeous, a damn good student, and out of her freaking mind." And the first time he had tried to cop a feel during one their sessions, she hadn't wasted her time telling him off. She had slugged him instead, and though her knuckles had ached for several days afterward, she hadn't felt the least bit guilty.

He had been fired two days later.

As for his opinion of her, she knew it was one held by more than a few. The "drop-dead gorgeous" part she wasn't too sure about. That she was pretty she already knew, without conceit; how much further that went depended, she supposed, on those who saw her. She had never let it get in her way.

She was also, for the most part, a pretty good student in whatever she put her mind to learn. That was, more than anything, a matter of pride. Despite the changing times, people who saw a woman like her, with rich and thick blond hair, automatically concluded she was dumb as a post. But she had long ago decided that the only person she had to prove anything to was herself; if she failed now and then, and she did, she couldn't accuse herself of not trying.

The "out of her freaking mind" was something else again. Without question, she knew that was pretty much accurate, and she actually liked it. If, that is, they were referring to the chances she liked to take as she searched for ways to find out just how far she could go without scaring herself to death.

She had been doing it for years, ever since she was a teen and some half-baked, so-called Southern gentleman had told her she had the perfect figure for motherin' and cookin', so why did she want to ruin all that by, of all things unwomanly on this man's earth, learning to drive in a NASCAR race.

She had taken strong exception.

And now that she was just past thirty, without children or marriage or very many regrets, the only true limit she had discovered was cave exploring. The idea that tons of rock and earth could slam down on her at any moment, without warning, and trap her, alone, in total darkness, had given her nightmares for a week after her first experience underground. Thinking it a common reaction for the initiate, she had tried it again, and again had nearly panicked.

A limit had been found; but only in one direction.

Today she was headed, in a sense, in a totally opposite one: today she would fly.

She loved it.

She loved the rush of wind against her face when she leapt off the mountain; she laughed aloud each time the wings that held her up shuddered against a gust and drove her muscles close to cramps as she forced the glider to do what she wanted; and she never landed without a shriek of sheer joy.

It didn't matter that she didn't do it very often. Her work, and her bank account, often conspired to hold the experience down to once or twice a month, if that. It didn't matter in the long run, however, because she desperately didn't want it to become ordinary.

She couldn't have stood that.

She couldn't have stood to lose the exhilaration.

In fact, her routine on flying days had been deliberately set to enhance that feeling: slow getting up, carefully filling time during the hours before flight by shopping or cleaning house, driving up Lookout Mountain at a pace that drove those who followed nuts, and sitting as she did now in the graveled parking area, watching others soar.

Leon's Air wasn't much of an operation, and not nearly as used at the other launch spot, a mile north along the ridge. But it had a feel to it she liked. It consisted of a large barnlike shed for storing rental equipment, the graveled parking area, and a five-foot concrete launch lip that extended over the edge of the drop.

There wasn't really room for much else.

The ridge here was only a hundred yards or so wide, barely accommodating the two-lane paved road that led back to the town of Lookout Mountain, some shrubs and trees on the east side, and Leon's place on the west. With the trees bare and the wind in constant motion, it often seemed as if she were walking on the edge of a two-sided cliff.

A man stepped out of the shed and waved.

She grinned and climbed out, the wind instantly taking her long blond hair and slapping it across her face.

"Hey," Leon Hendean said. "Happy almost New Year." He was tall, heavy without the fat, and bearded.

A bear who spoke quietly and gently . . . when he spoke at all.

Trish shivered as December cold slipped under her clothes, and thought, only for a moment, that maybe she'd picked a bad day. The sky was overcast, the wind a bit strong, and she was, for the time being, the only one here.

Sunset was only an hour away.

She made her way to the concrete lip and looked out over the valley. Nearly two thousand feet below she could see broad patches of green—some were farms, at least two were landing sites for the two hang-gliding operations. The rest of the land was heavily wooded, broken only by a winding two-lane road that ran north and south. What she couldn't see was the storage shed below Leon's, the truck used to cart flyers and equipment back up the mountain, and the van that doubled as an ambulance in case of an accident.

Her hands fisted in her flight-jacket pockets.

"You going?" he asked, a few steps behind her.

It was weird—he ran this place, a growing favorite among those who liked to pretend they were eagles, but he never stood close to the edge. Trish, on the other hand, delighted in it, checking the area for emergency landing spots while knowing that, except for the valley floor, there were none. The mountainside was choked with rocks, trees, and brush, and for a good third of its height, it was vertical.

She had long ago conquered that unbearable feeling of wanting to let go, to just fall. Flying was a better way to get to the ground.

"What do you think?" she said, stepping back to stand beside him.

"Strong, but not impossible."

"Am I the first?"

He shook his head. "Had a bunch around noon, before the clouds came in. No reports."

No updrafts, no sheers, no abrupt changes in wind speed.

"Then what the hell, Leon." She poked his arm. "Besides, it's my century."

His grin made her smile. She had promised him a date on her hundredth flight, and was pleased he had remembered.

"Supergirl," was all he said, however, and she spent the next twenty minutes preparing for the jump, double-checking the equipment she knew he had already checked a dozen times that day, pulling on an insulated, modified flight suit to protect her against the cold, setting helmet and goggles, and making sure the bag into which her legs would be tucked was safely affixed to the glider's frame by its harness.

Stretching exercises to ease her muscles while, at the same time, they prepared her mind to accept the fact that she was about to deliberately jump off the side of a mountain.

She barely remembered Leon helping her into the frame, hooking the harness, giving her a thumbs-up, bringing her to the edge.

She barely remembered the *please God* prayer.

She barely remembered the launch itself, concentrating instead on testing the wind as she swooped down the mountainside, then swooped up sharply until she was level with the shed's roof. She heard nothing but the wind, the snap of the glider's canopy wings, and her own muffled cries of delight as she banked to the left and began the downward spiral.

It was cold.

Too cold.

Despite her gloves, her fingers were freezing.

This was her least favorite kind of flying—taking herself all too quickly to the landing area. But she had underestimated the cold, and knew that if she wanted one more chance to play tag with the birds today, she wouldn't be able to take her time this time.

The valley shifted lazily, and all the noise was reduced to silence.

She was alone.

Out of her freaking mind with the indescribable, almost sexual feeling, of flying without natural wings.

That euphoria had, on more than one occasion, made her weep.

It also was a constant threat to her concentration, and she was startled when, five hundred feet down, a gust sideswiped her, driving her closer to the mountain wall.

She shifted legs and arms expertly and swung away, and down, and was caught again, this time taking her to the left, parallel to the trees that blurred past her.

Well, hell, she thought. She would have to gain some distance and dive a little. The wind wanted her to stay up, and the mountain wanted to take her. Not for the first time. A hazard of the sport.

Suddenly everything calmed and her speed decreased, and she was able to relax, just a little. Now, as she swung north again, she could see the details of the mountain's west face, truly gliding now instead of racing. Once, she had seen a family of deer picking its way across a clearing; once, not too long ago, she had seen something else, a dark creature she couldn't identify and hadn't seen again. A bear, maybe, something like that.

Now she was flying.

Tension eased, and at a thousand feet she wondered if she could take a wide arc around the landing area instead of heading straight in. The clouds had already thickened; no chance she'd be able to go up again.

What would it hurt?

A decent flight now, and a longer flight later with Leon.

What could it hurt?

A flock of crows exploded from the trees to her right, out of the mountain, startling her as they flew overhead, and below her. At the same time, another gust, slapping her this time from above.

Something snapped.

She heard it, and her mouth dried instantly.

She felt it when the glider refused to obey her command to get the hell over there, down there to the green patch where now she could see the shed, and the truck, and the ambulance van.

Oh, God, please, she thought, searching the area just below for a safe place to land in case she couldn't regain control; please.

The glider took her down.

Slowly, but too fast.

Her left arm ached, her gloved fingers almost released their grip on the crossbar, and for a wild, almost hysterical moment she was glad she had brought her own personal body bag with her—all they'd have to do when they found her was zip it up and cart her off.

The trees were too close.

A small clearing, canted and brown, broke the solid woodland wall.

Only chance, girl, she told herself, and headed straight for it.

Landing would be a bitch, she'd be lucky to break

only a leg or two, but if she hit it dead center, she wouldn't break her neck against one of those trees.

Something snapped.

Trish fell, wings fluttering above her as she freed her legs, and braced herself to hit.

When she did, the fire in her ankles, her legs, her hips, drove her into the dark.

When consciousness returned, she was tangled face down in the frame, and she giggled when she realized she was alive. Broken all the hell up, but still alive. As long as she didn't move, Leon's valley people would find her. She knew that. He always followed his flyers with binoculars, radio in one hand, ready to transmit locations. Just in case.

"Okay," she said aloud, just to hear her voice. "Okay."

A test of her arms brought agony from her right leg, but it nothing she couldn't handle, and she wanted the damn frame off the back of her neck. Carefully, grunting, once screaming quietly, she managed to wriggle free.

There was no wind down here.

All she could hear was the sound of the crows.

She giggled again and, bracing for pain, lifted herself up on her elbows and looked around through the veil of her hair.

This time the scream was loud.

It didn't last very long.

5

The early January night was raw, sometimes windy. Streetlights were brittle, footfalls sharp, and even a whisper sounded much too loud. The stars were gone, and light snow was promised over the city by morning.

Richard closed his eyes briefly; there was something more in the air.

A watcher.

Unseen, but out there, somewhere in the shadows.

His three-room apartment was in an old and small, undistinguished complex in Arlington. Although he was seldom there for more than a couple of weeks at a time, he had long ago come to a simple and effective arrangement with his landlady: she received treble the normal rent, and in return he was given unquestioning, absolute privacy—especially when he wasn't there.

And because he liked her and wished her no harm, the day he took possession, he had added enough security measures at the door and windows to defeat a small army. Like the cat, curiosity would have killed her.

So far it had worked for almost eight years.

Now he stood at the living-room window, staring down at the empty street, one hand absently massaging the side of his neck. The holiday decorations were gone, from the streetlamps and from the houses across the way. The trees were bare. No cars were parked at the curbs.

Not a sound out there, and no movement at all.

Still, there was something out there.

He tapped a finger on the sill, a monotonous rhythm that quickly got on his nerves.

Something in the air.

He growled softly, almost a humming.

Perhaps it was time for him to take a late stroll around the block. The neighborhood wouldn't complain; he had made it a habit to let himself be noticed when he went out after sunset, just another fitness nut, out there walking off the pounds no matter what the weather was.

The telephone rang.

He started at the noise, then laughed at himself as he pushed a nervous hand back through his hair. You're getting jumpy, he scolded, took one last look outside, and dropped onto the lumpy couch which, like all the other pieces of old, unmatched furniture, he had picked up from the previous tenant. One easy chair, a scarred side table, a standing brass lamp with a dark linen shade, a bookcase on the far wall, a thick wood shelf over his head on which perched a stone statuette of a night hawk, wings spread, eyes narrow.

The hawk was his.

"Richard?"

His smile broadened. "Fay? Is that you?"

"None other." Her voice was husky, almost masculine.

He looked across the unlighted room at the bookcase. He ignored the magazines and handful of books, concentrating instead on a niche that contained a two-foot high, blond-wood carving of a great horned owl.

"So what's up?"

"They need to see you."

He nodded, not bothering to add, *it's about time.* "When? Same place?"

"Yes. Tomorrow afternoon. Four."

"Okay, I'll be gone first thing. So how are you, Fay? It's been—"

"There's no time, Richard," she said, oddly impatient. "Just be there. And Richard . . . be careful."

She hung up.

He stared at the receiver for a second before replacing it in its cradle, then looked back at the owl.

A gust slapped at the window, causing the glow from the streetlamp to shimmer, and in shimmering, shifted shadows that made the bird's wings seem to move.

"What?" he asked softly. "What?"

In a desert whose mountains were made of sand, whose sky was streaked with light and dark shades of green that roiled like clouds in an unfelt storm, he made his way through the ruins of a temple, or a mansion that once belong to a king—pillars on their sides, snapped in half or snapped off at the base, only a handful still standing, holding nothing up but the sky; portions of walls against which sand had been banked by the constant furnace wind; statuary whose faces had been scoured blind; shards of bowls and urns.

There was heat, but he couldn't feel it.

He never had.

He had been here before, not just in his dreams.

A sudden gust punched his spine and he stumbled forward, awkwardly catching himself against a crumbling, waist-high wall before he fell. On it, faded by the unseen sun, chipped by falling rock, were hieroglyphs. He didn't look at them, didn't need to. They comprised a fragment of a much longer tale, the story of his people and the battle that had finally forced them out of the land of the Lower Nile.

Another gust forced him backward, half turning him around.

A third made him duck his head and move on, skirting a table tipped onto its side, nearly tripping through an empty doorway with no walls on either side.

The wind blew more strongly.

The sand didn't move.

He smelled fire and burning tar.

He heard his own breathing, rough and shallow, as he tried to keep his balance against the wind and the soft, shifting sands.

Through rooms and courtyards until finally he saw a fluted pedestal as high as his chest, standing alone in a wasteland of rocks and rocky sand. Its top was round and wide, its sides streaked with stains that could have been rust, could have been blood.

He walked around it slowly, frowning, reaching out to dust the pitted marble with his fingertips.

He had no idea what this was, or what it once held, until his left foot kicked something buried at the base. He leaned over and saw a streak of black, carefully brushed the sand away and blinked once, slowly.

It took both hands to lift the three-foot statue from the ground, and his face was streaked with perspiration as he placed it on the pedestal.

Anubis, exquisitely fashioned in onyx, every detail clear despite the complete absence of color.

The jackal-headed god stood with one foot slightly behind the other, teeth slightly bared, eyes slightly narrowed.

Its left hand was raised shoulder-high, palm out.

Its right arm was raised over its head, but it stopped at the elbow.

The rest was gone.

He backed away from it slowly, scowling as he scanned the ground for signs of the missing limb. He didn't know what the god had been holding in its other hand, and he didn't care. The fact that it had been mutilated was enough to make him nervous.

The green sky darkened.

The wind began to scream through holes in the rock.

Something told him to leave, now.

And something else made him watch as Anubis turned its head toward him and opened its jaws.

Richard sat up abruptly, eyes wide, mouth open in a shout that never made it past a moan caught in his throat. His gaze snapped around the bedroom, half expecting to see an intruder waiting in ambush deep in the shadows. But there was nothing but the dresser, the closet door, and the first faint light of dawn slowly filling the window.

"Damn," he whispered, and swallowed heavily. "Damn."

Wearily he dropped back onto the sweat-damp pillow and stared at the ceiling. The apartment was cool, he liked it that way, and it helped to drive away the remaining fragments of the nightmare even as he tried to figure out what it meant.

The ruins had been part of his dreamscape for

years; most of the time they signified little, if anything, beyond the reminder of what his people had
once had, and had lost. Every so often, however, the
scene was altered, and every so often he found
something he needed to know.

But he had never been afraid of them before.

Never.

He lay still for another minute, calming his
breathing, clearing his mind, before ruefully deciding there was no chance he'd be able to find sleep
again. Slowly he sat up again, and slid his legs over
the edge of the bed. He scratched his chest and
scalp vigorously, shook his head quickly, and moved
to the window to check the street.

Under an overcast sky a car crawled east; the old
man from up the street walked his yapping, mostly
hair, dog; two kids on bikes delivered papers.

Nothing he hadn't seen a hundred times before.

Whoever had been watching last night was gone,
and he still couldn't figure out if it had been a threat
or not.

He waited a few minutes longer, just to be sure,
then spent the next hour preparing for his trip across
the state to the outskirts of Roanoke. He wouldn't be
back soon. The summons Fay Parnell had given him
told him that much.

What he still didn't know was why she had broken
off their conversation so abruptly. He had known her
for several years, and for a brief and dangerous time
they had been lovers. Mystery was, of course, a part
of her allure, but he had never known her to show
the slightest bit of fear.

Yet there had definitely been fear in her voice the
night before.

For him, he wondered, or for herself?

He grunted sharply in a scold. Speculation was

useless, and at this stage it would only get him into trouble. Not, he thought wryly as he dressed, that trouble and he were strangers. Not only was it part of his job, but he also managed to get into enough of it on his own, without any help from outsiders. He knew full well that impulse and instinct were often necessary to his survival; he also knew that once in a while, despite his best efforts, they stampeded reason, and left him scrambling for solid ground.

Whenever you feel the urge, Fay had once told him with a smug, friendly grin, *count to five before you walk off the damn cliff, okay? And be sure you have a parachute.*

The trouble with that was, by the time he remembered the advice, he was sometimes already on the way down.

Without the damn parachute.

Another grunt, this one more like a laugh, and once packed—a small cloth bag, nothing more, that he would keep on the seat beside him—he activated the apartment's elaborate security measures, pulled on a fleece-lined leather jacket, and stood before the owl.

Tell me, he asked it silently; tell me what you see.

Then he sighed and left, stopping in the large, once elegant lobby to knock on Mrs. Allantero's door. She answered immediately, as he knew she would. The woman never slept, and no one ever left the building without her somehow knowing about it.

She wore ancient slippers, and an oversize floral dress that made her look heavier than she really was. As it was, she barely came up to the middle of his chest. A squint at his bag over the top of her reading glasses: "You going away?"

"For a while, yes."

She nodded. "You be good, Richard. The world's going to hell out there."

He grinned. "I'll take care, don't worry."

She didn't ask when he would be back, didn't even blink when he handed her an envelope that contained the next four months' rent. It disappeared somewhere into the folds of her dress. Then she reached around the door, and handed him a brown paper lunch bag, stuffed with cookies and, probably, an orange and an apple. It was another of their rituals; he seldom left town without one of her trip-snacks.

A quick good-bye, then, and he hurried outside, around the corner of the building to the side parking lot as he shivered against the unexpected damp cold. His car was purposely nondescript and looked as if it should have been traded in a dozen years ago. Yet it felt like a favorite glove—not pretty, but it fit him perfectly. It warmed up quickly, and as he pulled into the street, he looked back and saw Mrs. Allantero in her window. Watching; always watching.

Her left hand lifted in a tentative wave, and he smiled and waved back.

Surrogate mother, he thought.

He wondered, then, what she would think if she knew her star tenant and surrogate son was actually a member of a race that called itself the Garou.

She wouldn't know what that meant.

But she would, without a doubt, recognize a were-wolf.

Shapes and shadows in the fog.

As the land rose toward the Blue Ridge Mountains, the clouds lowered, and across the increasing number of pastures and fields, pockets of mist and fog rose from creeks and streams, and crept out of the woodland. By Roanoke, shortly before sunset, most of the summits were buried in ragged gray, and thin, gray patches had slipped across the road.

Richard was uneasy.

Just like the night before, he couldn't shake the feeling that there was something out there, pacing him—flashes of dark movement in the fog, a breeze-caused rip in the mist to reveal something standing in a meadow, the sense of something on the highway behind him, keeping out of sight just around the last bend.

It was foolish.

It was probably an understandable combination of being summoned again after so long a layoff, the nightmare, and Fay's inexplicable warning. A touch of imagination, a dash of paranoia; he was lucky he wasn't seeing UFOs land on the highway.

Nevertheless, the shapes and shadows were out

there, and he was more than a little relieved when he crossed over Interstate 81 west of Roanoke and, a mile-and-a-half later, took a little-used side road down into a narrow valley where night was only a few minutes away. Open land had given way to trees and dense brush, the side road to his destination practically buried behind tall reeds hiding a shallow, wide creek on the right.

As always, he drove past it twice to be sure no one had followed, then took the right turn slowly onto a single-lane road, and stopped almost immediately. He checked the rearview mirror, rubbed his chin, and finally got out, trailing one hand along the car's side as he walked to the back bumper and checked the main road in both directions.

Just be to sure again.

Nothing.

And nothing in the thick woods across the way, nothing in the sky below the clouds.

Maybe, he thought, and not for the first time recently; maybe I'm getting a little too old for this game.

As he turned to get back into the car, a flurry of crows exploded noisily out of the trees across the road, spinning dead leaves and alarms in their wake. He spun instantly into a crouch, cocking his head to listen as the flock's cries faded into the hillsides, straining to find movement in the twilight beneath the branches.

Most the trees were pine, but there were gaps he could see through, and shadows that dipped and wavered as a breeze slipped out of the woods into his face.

Slowly, uncertain, he rose and crossed the road, sidestepped down and up the mossy sides of a shallow ditch, and made his way in.

A crow called in the distance.

It could have been a deer, a bear, but their recognizable scents were not in the air; the birds could have spooked themselves, but he didn't think so.

He moved around a gnarled, half-dead pine, letting the lower branches glide off his left arm and shoulder.

Above him, the breeze had kicked into a wind, soughing, scattering leaves, snapping off dead twigs. Good and bad: it would mask his own movement, but he wouldn't be able to hear anyone else's.

Another ten yards that took him ten minutes.

Pine needles on the ground matted into strips of brown and dull green; the nearly flat body of a long-dead squirrel lying beneath a laurel; a small pool of black, stagnant water that rippled thickly when the wind touched the surface.

He saw no prints, caught no spoor, and was about to give himself a swift mental kick in the butt, when he saw something quivering in a bush off to his right.

The branches, thick and dark gray, were horned, and a small piece of cloth struggled near the bottom. He pulled it off between thumb and forefinger, held it close to his eyes, then squinted into the wind. Still no prints, but this time he had the scent.

Human.

And long gone.

There was still a chance Richard might catch him—whoever it was had probably bolted when the crows took flight—but there was no time.

And for the moment, there was no danger.

Still, he waited a few minutes more, just in case, before returning to the car and rattling over a narrow wood bridge in serious need of repair. The road beyond was mostly stone and potholes, a deliberate discouragement to the casual weekend explorer.

A quarter of a mile later he reached a broad clearing and took his foot off the accelerator, letting the car roll to a silent stop.

*   *   *

The house, despite its size, was not very imposing. It had been constructed to follow the top arc of the long circular drive that fronted it, yet it didn't seem to be that large. Towering firs on the slopes behind and away on its flanks shrank the single-story brick and white-trim building, and even its one-acre front yard with its evergreen shrubs and now barren gardens looked little bigger than a postage stamp. The eagle weather vane in the center of the peaked roof, its brass dull without sunshine, quivered. Carriage lamps on either side of the paneled, double-front doors were lit, but the amber glass seemed less welcoming than cold. All the windows were blinded by closed draperies.

Had that casual weekend explorer gotten this far, he would have sworn, despite the lights, that the place was deserted.

Richard frowned his bemusement when he realized there were no cars parked on the drive. There should have been. Six or seven, at least. A spur off to the right led to an old stable converted into a six-car garage. The three that he could see were open, and there were no vehicles in there either.

He checked his watch, and the frowned deepened momentarily. He wasn't late, and he doubted the others were, either. He would learn the reason for their absence soon enough.

He parked just past the entrance and opened the car door, shivering slightly at the chill that ruffled across his face. A good feeling. The scent of fir and pine, the scent of untainted air—a good feeling that would do until he was given the reason for the summons.

He glanced at the darkening sky, and the clouds were lower still.

A crow called from the woods, and was answered by another, coasting beneath the clouds.

The wind sent a single leaf spiraling over the roof.

Richard watched it vanish behind the weather vane, and shook his head. He had never really liked this place. It was too isolated, too vulnerable. A glance over his shoulder, a scowl into the wind. That human, whoever he was, might be in there, in the trees, either watching and nothing more, or fixing the sights of a rifle on his head.

"Enough," he told himself angrily. There was always the possibility it had only been a hunter or a hiker; it wasn't necessary to turn every shadow into something sinister.

Yet Fay had said, be careful when there shouldn't have been anything to be careful of at all.

He was almost tempted to walk around to the back to do some checking on his own, but the temptation faded quickly, and he slipped his right hand into his trouser pocket, fingers closing around a small cloth bag. He squeezed it once, for luck and reassurance, then strode cautiously to the front door.

Unlike his previous visits, there was no sign of greeting.

None at all.

Suddenly, ridiculously, he felt like the heroine in an old suspense movie—she and the audience knew full-well there was danger on the other side of that door, and contrary to all reason, she opened it anyway.

She and the audience were always right.

"Damn," he muttered. This was stupid. What the hell was the matter with him?

. . . *be careful* . . .

He took a slow deep breath and knocked.

The right-hand door opened immediately, soundlessly.

He started, cursed himself for the reaction, and stepped inside without waiting for an invitation, nodding once to a middle-aged woman dressed in a severe, expensive brown suit, no flourishes at all, her solid brown hair tightly caught in a bun at her nape.

"Afternoon, Hester," he said pleasantly. "Will you tell them I'm here?"

Not a smile in return, just a sharp commanding nod that told him to stay where he was.

He didn't argue.

The foyer was large, with a polished flagstone floor and undecorated white walls split by exposed beams. Dim light fell from a small teardrop chandelier in the center of the ceiling. At the back, sliding glass doors overlooked a yard nearly the size of a football field, mostly brown now, and spotted at the back with shaded patches of snow that must have fallen the night before. In the middle of the walls right and left were entries to corridors he knew ran the length of the house, all the rooms opening off them, a curious arrangement he had never bothered to question.

No one lived here.

As far as he knew, no one even stayed here overnight. Not even Hester Darchek.

The foyer was too warm. He unzipped his coat, then slipped it off and draped it over his left shoulder, moved it from there to drape over his right arm. He walked to the glass doors and stared at the yard, walked back to the entrance and stared at the tips of his shoes, tried counting the bulbs in the chandelier, and decided that if he didn't do something soon, he was going to drive himself crazy.

Hester returned a minute later, beckoned once, and he followed her into the hall on the right, its thick floral carpeting smothering their footsteps. Again, there was no ornamentation on the walls, the only light from candle-shaped bulbs beneath milk-glass chimneys in sconces beside each dark-wood door they passed.

Not a sound.

Not even the rising wind.

He wanted to whistle something, anything, just to break the silence, but he had a feeling Hester wouldn't approve; he also had a feeling, without really knowing why, that he wouldn't be very happy if he ever sparked her ire.

Still . . . it was tempting.

Halfway along, the woman paused just long enough to gesture him to an open door before she headed back toward the foyer, hands clasped at her stomach.

Richard smiled pleasantly as she passed, and rolled his eyes when, as usual, there was no response.

In all the time he had known her, if "known" was the word, she had never spoken more than a few words at a time, never smiled, never broken the indifferent mask she wore.

A deep voice with a touch of an English accent said, "Do come in, Richard, come in."

The room was a full twenty-five feet on a side, the walls papered white-and-rose on top, with dark walnut wainscoting below. A carved oak sideboard stood to the left just inside the door, and in the center was a gleaming refectory table large enough to seat eighteen.

There were no windows or other exits.

There were no lamps; the only illumination came from hooded bulbs embedded in the ceiling, one for each of the eighteen chairs. All else was in deep shadow.

There were only three others in the room.

Instantly, Richard felt all his defenses go up.

There should have been, at the very least, nine or ten men and women here.

His first thought was, Jesus, it's a trap.

7

The man seated at the head gave him a half-smile. "Welcome, my friend," and nodded Richard to the low, heavy chair at the foot of the table.

Richard didn't accept the invitation. He moved to the offered chair, but remained on his feet, gripping the bowed top lightly. The door was still open, and he made no move to close it.

He didn't have to; it closed on its own seconds after he touched his chair.

"Richard, are you well?"

"Well enough, John."

Even seated, John Chesney was tall, with sharp planes and deep shadows in his face that made him appear as if a lifetime of dissipation had caught up with him overnight. His hair was thick, pure white, and brushed straight back had gotten from the movies. He also supposed Chesney believed it lent him an air of authority.

He didn't need it.

He had eyes that could boil blood if he ever lost his temper.

To Richard's right, beside Chesney, was Maurice

Poulard, a stocky man with a florid, pudgy face that
left little room for his eyes. His gray suit looked like
silk; his red club tie undoubtedly was. He was bald;
deliberately bald. In his right hand he held a lace-
edged handkerchief he used to mop his scalp, to
wave a point, and to touch to his oddly thin lips
whenever he wanted to hide what his mouth might
reveal. He waved the handkerchief now, his voice
reed-thin: "Oh, do sit, Richard. We're not going to
bite, you know."

The woman on his left laughed silently. She wore
a tailored burgundy suit, a ruffled cream blouse, and
a huge ruby ring on her left hand. Her hair was short
and brushed back over her ears, a style that suited
her ageless features. She could have been thirty,
could have been sixty, but apparently that didn't
matter to those reputed to be her lovers. "You're
confused, dear," she said, her voice soothing and
smooth.

He nodded. "I am, Vi."

"Then sit. Please. John has things to tell you, and
we don't have much time."

"The others?" he asked as he obeyed.

Poulard waved the handkerchief dismissively.
"Not here, not coming."

Richard almost said, that's impossible, but the
look on the man's face stopped him.

He had been right—he shouldn't have knocked,
he shouldn't have come in.

This was the chamber of the Warders of the Veil.
Seldom used, but when it was, it held a representa-
tive of most of the thirteen tribes of the Garou.

Never just three.

Never.

His unease increased as he waited for Chesney
to make up his mind when to begin. The man was

an actor. Nothing he did was done without consideration of its dramatic effect, including the annoying, overhead lighting. It was he who had named the group, he—along with Viana Jaye, Maurice, and two others now dead—who had seen the need, and he who had recruited Richard into their midst.

The reason, in the beginning, had been simple and right: Gaia was dying, and along with her, the Garou.

The Earth, in spite of the best efforts of some, had begun to flounder in the aftermath of steadily increasing populations. Urban centers expanded with little planning, waste was more stockpiled than converted for reuse, and what was once pristine had become irrevocably soiled.

The Garou, because they were so intricately involved with the system that supported both Man and Gaia, thus found themselves in danger as well. Their numbers had never been that great in the first place; now each of the tribes found themselves much smaller, with less protection, fewer chances of survival.

The Veil was that which separated men from the Garou. For men, Richard and the others were the stuff of legends and tales told around campfires— werewolves. Man-beasts. Evil creatures that stalked movie screens and novels and children's nightmares in autumn. As long as it remained that way, the Garou could manage, doing what they could to keep Gaia from collapsing.

When the Veil was lifted, however, and however briefly and accidentally, something had to be done.

The Warders had been created when it was evident that recent breaches of the Veil weren't accidental at all.

Chesney put his glass down and cleared his throat.

Richard glanced at the others, leaned back, and said with a brief smile, "John, I'm falling asleep."

Vi laughed; Maurice scowled.

Chesney at least had the grace to look embarrassed, caught in his own acting. He folded his hands on the table and cleared his throat again. "Richard," he said, "there's a rogue."

Two vicious murders in Tennessee, near Chattanooga and the Georgia border, and at least two more missing, Chesney explained. Even discounting the natural hysteria in the media concerning such brutal and puzzling acts, it was clear to the Warders that a rogue had moved into the area, and he had to be stopped before the police caught him.

Richard didn't respond; it wasn't expected of him.

Every so often, it happened: a Garou from any tribe could break under the pressure of either living in both worlds, or keeping his pact to protect Gaia. In this way, they were no different from humans—they had their weak links, and sometimes they snapped.

It was his job to make sure the rogue was never caught, dead or alive, by humans. If he failed, the truth of the Garou would be out; it didn't take a genius to figure out what would happen then.

So far, he hadn't failed.

But what he still didn't understand was why the full group wasn't here. The first known attack had been back in October, the latest only last week, the disappearances sometime between. Someone should have been investigating from the first killing—plenty of time to convene a strategy session, and to contact him. Waiting this long to suspect a rogue . . .

Still, he held his peace. While the others were of tribes whose lives revolved around packs, he was called Silent Strider. His kind were loners. Travelers. As such, and as now, most of the other Garou either held them in mild contempt, or outright distrust that sometimes bordered on fear.

A wolf, alone, wasn't natural.

Rogues they could understand; someone like Richard they couldn't.

Vi dusted a finger across the tabletop. "There's more, of course."

He smiled at her wryly. "I'd be surprised if there wasn't."

"Oh, for God's sake," Poulard snapped. "Get on with it. I'm a busy man." His handkerchief flapped at the others. "This is getting us nowhere."

Chesney's face darkened briefly, his eyes narrowing as he turned toward Poulard and silently demanded he hold his tongue. Poulard snarled but sat back, almost pouting.

Well, Richard thought; well, well.

Chesney turned his attention back to Richard, all signs of displeasure gone in a blink. "You know there are humans who suspect who and what we are."

Richard nodded impatiently. He didn't need, nor did he appreciate, a history lesson. Yes, there were humans who suspected what lay beyond the Veil; yes, some had actually begun to accumulate evidence of it; and yes, some had the potential to be more than a small threat to the Garou's existence. But they didn't work together; they didn't share what they knew. All had their own agendas, and so far, luckily, cooperation hadn't been part of it.

"Well, there's something else," Chesney said, and hesitated. Vi whispered something Richard couldn't catch, and the older man nodded. "The rogue. We think he might be a trap. We . . . think he's out there, specifically, to lure you into the open."

"Somebody wants you dead, Richard," Vi said.

"Or more likely," Poulard added impatiently, and without much sympathy, "somebody wants you in hand so you can lead them to us." He folded the handkerchief into a rectangle on the table and carefully smoothed out its wrinkles with the side of his hand. "It is also possible that this someone is one of us."

"No," he said without having to think. He looked at the others. "That's impossible."

Poulard stared at him without raising his head. "Is it, Richard? Is it really?"

"Of course it is," he said automatically.

The tribes, while all Garou, weren't always in harmony. They had their common goal, but the means to achieve it were often sources of dissension, and causes of rivalries that in some cases were generations old.

But nothing like this.

No matter how bad relations got, tribes didn't go to war with one another.

Not at the risk of rending the Veil.

He shifted uncomfortably when no one reacted. "Who told you this nonsense?"

No one answered.

He shook his head in disgust and stared at the wood surface immediately in front of him. Despite the high polish, there was no reflection, just the grain. It didn't give him any answers, or any inspiration.

"This rogue," Chesney said quietly, "has to be brought back, I'm afraid."

That snapped Richard's head up. "What?"

It was difficult enough to hunt down one of your

own kind, one who had been overcome by rage-filled madness; the outcome was always the same. It had to be. There was no cure for the sickness that created a rogue, and no safe way or place to detain him. But to say that he had to be captured was madness of its own.

"There's no other way. We need to know, Richard. We need to know."

Poulard pushed his chair away from the table, to the edge of the reach of his light. He leaned back and folded his hands over his stomach. "It's quite simple. You do what you always do, Richard, except that you don't kill him." He smiled without humor. "Do you think you can handle that?"

"That's not the point," he said.

"Oh, but it is." The smile remained. "Unless you don't feel that you can. Succeed, that is. Feeling a little old these days?"

Richard looked to Vi, but she too had retreated, and all he could see of her without straining were her hands and her torso. It was as if someone had suddenly cut off her head.

"That's not the point either, Maurice," he said, struggling to keep his temper intact. "But if I'm even going to consider this . . . this assignment, I'll need to know more." He looked directly at Chesney. "Like, who else I'll be up against, if what you say is true."

"Unknown," was all Chesney answered.

"Then why do you suspect it may be one of us?"

"Our privilege," Poulard said quickly.

Right, Richard thought; catch a rogue, but wear a blindfold while you're at it, and don't worry about your back, you don't need to know who's got the knife.

Chesney coughed lightly into a fist. "You'll have to leave tonight, Richard. We can't waste any more time arguing. Or," he added pointedly to Maurice, "speculating. Just bring us what we ask."

"And if I can't?"

Vi slipped back into the light. "I fear, Richard, that's not an option in this case." She spread her hands. "I'm sorry."

"And if I can't," he persisted.

"We'll get someone else," Poulard answered blithely.

Richard inhaled slowly, but said nothing more. It was an empty threat. He knew as well as Maurice did that there was no one else. The Warders were select. The only way he could be replaced was if he was killed.

Still . . . "Well, if you do, Maurice, be sure to let him know that someone's been poking around out here."

"What?" It was Poulard's turn to slip back into the light. "What are you talking about?"

Richard gestured vaguely over his shoulder. "It may be nothing, but I've had the feeling all day that someone's been following me." He reached into his jacket pocket and tossed the ragged swatch onto the table. "I found this just before I arrived."

Poulard slammed a palm on the table. "You irresponsible son of a bitch! Why didn't you say anything when you got here?"

"Because he's gone, Maurice," he answered calmly.

Chesney stared down the length of the table at the piece of cloth. "How do you know, Richard?"

"Because I do, John."

Poulard mopped his scalp nervously. "And you didn't go after him?"

"I had been summoned, remember?"

"And the danger?"

Richard's voice flattened; the fat man was rapidly getting on his nerves. "If there had been danger, I would have ended it." He had had enough. He stood, picked up the swatch and his jacket, and held out his left hand. "John?"

Chesney hesitated before taking an envelope from an inside pocket and sliding down the table. Richard picked it up, folded it, and stuffed it into his hip pocket, the move deliberately casual, just to taunt Poulard. Then he pushed his chair aside and strode to the door, opened it, and turned around when Vi said his name.

"You'll do it, won't you?"

"Like I said, Vi—if I can." But he relented when he saw her stricken expression. "Don't worry. Anything else will only be a last resort."

He stepped into the hallway.

The door closed silently behind him.

For a long moment he didn't move. He could hear raised voices in the chamber, Poulard's in argument, Chesney's snapping. A trickle of ice touched the length of his spine.

That wasn't simple rivalry in there.

He didn't need extra senses to know it was fear.

There were no shapes or shadows now; the night had taken them, and had replaced them with long stretches of nothing but the reach of the old car's headlamps, turning the tarmac gray, blending the trees along the highway into a mottled, black wall.

He almost made it to Knoxville before weariness overtook him, abrupt and unexpected. It less on the early start and all the driving he'd done, and the startling realization that he had been barely aware of the road since leaving Virginia.

Neither the interstate's sparse evening traffic nor the darkened landscape had registered except as flashes of headlights, glimpses of illuminated signs pointing this way to fuel, that way to food.

He had been functioning on automatic, his concentration focused on trying to understand what had really happened at the curious meeting with the Warders. It wasn't only the assignment—bring the rogue back alive—it had also been almost as if they wanted him in there and gone with as little fuss and discussion as possible.

That wasn't like them.

Most of the time, similar meetings took at least two or three hours, while ramifications were debated, reasons for a Garou's turning rogue were offered, sides were taken, and demands were made. To a virtual outsider like him, they were almost comical, and would have been had they not been so potentially dangerous for his kind.

But today had been nothing short of unnerving.

Currents and undercurrents.

And not a single mention of Fay.

He yawned suddenly, and so widely and noisily that he laughed aloud and decided Chattanooga could wait until morning. He needed to sleep before he wound up wrapped against a tree, or nose-down in a ditch.

He found a Ramada Inn half a mile off the highway just east of Knoxville, and took a room. He had barely set his bag down on a low and long chest of drawers when he began to pace from door to window, over and over. As soon as he caught himself doing it, he went outside, to walk for a while, to stretch his limbs and breathe the night air.

Despite the weariness, he was restless, too restless to stay in a place with four walls.

The two-story motel was on a knoll, surrounded by a parking lot that seemed like a moat between the building itself and the woodland around it. The nearest community was a few miles farther north, and the still-hovering cloud cover reflected no lights at all.

With his jacket open and his hands in his pockets, he walked the perimeter slowly, smelling the pine, the cedar, the earth still damp from a recent light rain. He heard muffled music drifting from the motel's bar, and from the rooms a voice raised in querulous complaint, someone laughing gently, someone slamming dresser doors; from the highway he heard the grumble of a truck.

He trotted a few steps, then walked again, keeping close to the trees in case someone should look out.

He wouldn't be seen; he was as much at home out here as he was in there.

His third circuit had just begun when he realized that the world had suddenly fallen silent.

He stopped and cocked his head, straining for a sound, any sound, beyond the rasp of his own breathing.

It lasted only a few seconds, but it was long enough to remind him, for reasons he couldn't immediately understand, that his restlessness wasn't entirely due to the disturbing Roanoke meeting.

Most of it, he realized, was because it been a while, much too long, since he had last hunted.

Since he had last taken the form.

Since he had last marked his prey.

Since he had last tasted blood.

A slow smile almost parted his lips. A rumbling in his throat almost tickled.

A glance at the building, few of the windows lighted, and he wondered what they would think if they heard something howling out here. Would they come out, or would they hide? Investigate, or call for help?

It was tempting, so wonderfully, dangerously tempting that he might have done it had not a first-floor drapery parted, and he could see a shadow there, someone looking out at the night.

He sighed for good sense, and headed back to his room.

Tomorrow, he promised himself; tomorrow night he would allow himself a few hours of freedom.

For now, however, there was rest to be taken, and maybe a quick call to Fay to find out where she had been, and what she had meant when she had warned him to be careful. But once in the room, he barely had time to take off his clothes before sleep dragged him onto the bed.

There was only one dream:

In the desert, in the ruins, the jaws of Anubis dripped blood.

A faint rumble of thunder echoed across the city, and a flare of pale lightning marked the horizon between the sky and the Pacific.

In the street, down in the Tenderloin, among the crowds, a trio of well-dressed drunks argued loudly and profanely, while a woman leaning against a lamppost laughingly shrieked for the police. The sidewalks and tarmac reflected the garish neon as if the rain had already arrived. A police car ghosted through, and no one paid it any mind.

A telephone rang, and Miles Blanchard groaned at the intrusion and rolled over, clamping the bed's other pillow over his head. When the ringing persisted, he cursed loudly, in several languages, as he flung the pillow aside and fumbled with the receiver, nearly dropping it to the floor. He cursed again and sat up, rubbing his eyes with his knuckles, demanding the caller's identification even before he put the receiver to his ear.

As soon as he heard the telltale high-pitched whine, however, he hung up and swung out of bed.

Within seconds he had the proper equipment attached and ready.

Exactly one minute later, the telephone rang again. The whine was gone, and he was wide awake.

"Mr. Blanchard."

"Yes, sir."

"Are you rested?"

Blanchard thought of the woman who had left not two hours ago, trailing a ratty mink stole behind her, and grinned at the empty room, barely clean enough not to be called seedy. Sometimes, he thought, you just had to make sacrifices.

"Are you rested, Mr. Blanchard?"

"Yes, sir, as well as I can be, sir." He hoped the innuendo hadn't been lost. Not that it would matter. Crimmins wouldn't care if Blanchard was a monk.

"Excellent. And your assignment?"

"Completed, sir, no problems at all. You'll have your report before sunset, as usual."

"Again, excellent."

The man scowled at the far wall, its dull floral paper waterstained near the ceiling. This call wasn't usual, and he didn't much care for the questions he had and knew he couldn't ask. As a matter of fact, the more he thought about it, the more he realized he couldn't recall Crimmins ever contacting him like this, without prior arrangement.

He didn't like the chill that suddenly crawled up his spine.

"Uh, sir, is there a problem?"

There was a pause, and Blanchard frowned again.

The thunder grew louder.

Lightning flared around the edges of the cheap heavy drapes that covered the room's single window.

"Mr. Blanchard, do you recall your stay in the South last autumn?"

He answered without hesitation: "Yes, sir, I certainly do."

No lie; it was the first time Crimmins had ever authorized a bonus.

"Well, Mr. Blanchard, it appears as if we now have a situation down there."

"Yes, sir."

"Leave immediately and take care of it, Mr. Blanchard. Do you understand me? Take care of it."

Blanchard grinned without humor. "You can count on me, sir. Is there something special . . . ?"

Again, the long silence.

He rubbed his chest with his free hand.

"He's coming, Mr. Blanchard."

"I'm sorry?"

"Pay attention, Mr. Blanchard," Crimmins snapped. "I said, he's coming."

Blanchard caught himself before he laughed aloud in delight; instead he raised a fist and punched the air. He didn't have to ask who, or how Crimmins knew. At last, at long last that damned Strider would be in his sights; would be his for the taking. "I'll leave on the first plane I can get."

"See that you do, Mr. Blanchard, see that you do."

Blanchard frowned—what the hell did that mean?

"And Mr. Blanchard, please understand me. This time there are no options."

The frown faded quickly. "There never are, sir, I know that."

"No, you don't understand. I'm not only talking about him, I'm talking about you."

Blanchard stiffened, but the phone went dead before he could respond. Angrily, he dismantled the equipment; in a rage, he prowled the tiny room, fists clenched, eyes narrowed. The man had threatened him; actually threatened him. Him. As if he were some pissant amateur, some goddamn water boy, some goddamn servant, for God's sake.

He yanked the drapes aside and stood in the window, glaring down at the neon blurred and softened by rain.

He stood there for over an hour.

He didn't move.

Not once.

Shapes and shadows.

"It isn't going to work."

"Of course it will, Maurice. You must have faith."

"There is no faith. There is only what is."

"Gaia will be displeased."

"Gaia is dying, and we're doing nothing to help Her."

"This is nothing?"

"Yes. It's nothing. The rogues increase, and there are too few to fight them. The Veil isn't permanent. One of these days, it's going to be nothing more than shreds."

"Which is why we have Richard."

"Viana, for someone so smart, so . . . mature . . . you are one of the most naive people I have ever met. That smug bastard is going to die, and for Gaia's sake, you don't have to look so pained. You agreed, just like the rest of us."

"I agreed, yes. That doesn't mean I have to like it."

"Well, I do."

"I know, Maurice. I know."

"I just hope it's soon. We don't have much time."

In a chair by the bedroom door sat a large stuffed panda, a green bow loose around its neck, its black button eyes gleaming faintly in the glow from a panda night-light in the bathroom. On the opposite

wall was an oil landscape, framed in scrolled dark
wood, highlights faintly glittering. Beneath the
painting was a king-size bed with a brass headboard
and solid wood footboard. Beside the bed was a
nightstand, with a stuffed pink alligator coiled
around a stubby pewter lamp and a French provin-
cial telephone.

The telephone rang.

A long-fingered hand reached out from beneath
the quilt, grabbed the receiver after several clumsy
attempts, and pulled it back under the covers.

"This had better be good."

"It is. He's coming."

"When?"

"Probably tomorrow."

"Goody. Can I go back to sleep now?"

"But—"

The hand reappeared, dropped the receiver onto
its cradle,

and vanished again.

Hunger.

There was nothing else but the hunger.

The river was dark, a rippling reflection of the clouds that sat motionless over the city. There was no traffic on the water, no sign of movement on the opposite bank or the inhabited hills that rose behind it.

Although the air wasn't cold, it still felt like snow.

Richard shifted uncomfortably.

He sat on a bench facing the embankment, hands deep in his topcoat pockets, an occasional gust sifting hair into his eyes. He had arrived in Chattanooga just before noon, checked into a third-floor room at the Read House, and waited for someone to make contact.

No one had.

There had been no message for him at the desk; none while he ate a late lunch in the hotel restaurant; none when he returned to the room to pace and grow impatient. Fay still wasn't home, and that didn't help his already fraying temper. He had been seconds shy of placing an angry call to Chesney when a bellman delivered an envelope.

The folded cream paper inside said nothing more than aquarium park and the bellman hadn't a clue

67

who had brought it; it had been left at the front desk, that's all he knew.

The park on the river was more a plaza than a park, with paving stones, a few benches, young trees barely tall enough to be worthy of the name. No one had been there when he had arrived, and he was the only one here now. On his left, the Tennessee Aquarium rose in contemporary design and dark brick, the only windows on the ground floor, where the entrance and gift shop were.

He shifted again, and tucked his chin into his coat.

He had been here over an hour—it was just past four-thirty—and the only life he had seen was a group of schoolchildren heading noisily inside, herded by a pair of young, harried teachers. A short while later, he heard traffic slowly building behind him on Broad Street, a wide four-lane boulevard that cut through the city's center, the south end ending at the aquarium park; the north end narrowing and forking as it approached Lookout Mountain.

Ten minutes, he thought sourly; I'll give them ten minutes.

Excited voices turned his head. The kids were finally leaving, their tour over, and a school bus coughed impatiently at the curb. One child raced away from the others toward the water, bundled in bright colors, mittens dangling from strings on his sleeves.

"Don't," warned Richard softly as the child waddled past him.

The little boy stopped, tilted his head, and grinned. "Fish," he declared, pointing at the aquarium. His cheeks and the tip of his nose were already red.

"Right."

"Fish," the boy said, pointing now at the river.

Richard shook his head. "Nope. Not today."

At that moment one of the teachers rushed up and scooped the child into her arms. Flustered, face drawn with anxiety, she scolded the boy softly for leaving the class and, in the same breath, thanked Richard for stopping him.

"No problem," he said with a smile. "He wants to learn, that's all."

"Fish!" the boy yelled happily as he was carried away. "No fish!"

Suddenly Richard felt very old indeed.

But not so old that he didn't hear the footfall behind him. He straightened just as a woman came around the bench and sat on the far end. She wore a long emerald coat and matching scarf, obviously chosen to set off her dark-red hair cut short and brushed back over her ears. Black gloves, black shoes, black purse on a thick strap over her right shoulder. He guessed her to be in her early thirties.

"Sorry I'm late," she said without looking at him. Her voice was soft, and her accent clearly marked her as from Tennessee. "I got tied up."

He said nothing.

She did look then, mild doubt in her expression. "Oh, God, you are Richard, aren't you?"

"What if I'm not?"

"Then I've just made a complete ass of myself."

He smiled crookedly, tempted to deny it just to see her blush, then nodded before saying, "All this is a bit melodramatic, isn't it? It would have been warmer in the hotel. And a whole lot less public."

Unconcerned, she shrugged and looked at the sky, at the river. "People meet here all the time. No big deal. It's not like the CIA is watching us, you know." She slipped a hand inside her coat, pulled out a large manila envelope sealed with clear tape and dropped it on the bench between them. "Here's some stuff in here you should look at soon as you can." As he reached for it, she added, "Copies, of course. Police reports, the Medical Examiner, stuff like that. A few of my own notes, just to get you started."

He didn't open it. Instead, he folded it in half and jammed it into his pocket. "How'd you get this?"

She shrugged again. "That's easy. I'm a cop."

With every assignment large or small came a local contact, someone paid to bring him information, to open doors where necessary, and to forget he ever existed when he finally left town. They were usually told he was Government, nothing else, and seldom tried to mine him for more; those few who did were easily, gently thwarted. When he was gone, however, they were watched by others, just in case the money they received wasn't enough of a guarantee.

That had only happened once.

The contact hadn't survived.

Neither had any of the contacts been Garou. The Warders had decided that might pose more problems than they were worth. It was bad enough they had to hunt one of their own down; asking one to help a Strider was asking for trouble.

Nor had a contact ever before been as intimately knowledgeable with the cases at hand as Detective Sergeant Joanne Minster.

Another first.

Richard wasn't at all sure he liked it.

Police, the best police, had unspoken loyalties beyond the reach of a lucrative, extracurricular job. They also tended to ask too many questions. The right questions. The questions he would not be able to answer without lying. And lies had to be kept track of, had to be covered with virtually every word he said.

He wondered, then, as he looked at her, and liking what he saw, if she actually knew.

"If you're going to stare," she said softly, slowly turning her face toward him, "do it so people will think you're either getting ready to pop the question, or that you're just smitten with my incredible earthy beauty."

A heartbeat later she grinned.

He couldn't help it; he laughed and shook his head in apology.

When she rose, he stood with her, and they headed for the street, her arm tucked around his.

It felt good, her closeness; it felt natural.

And that, too, disturbed him.

He was used to being alone, that was his nature. Lately, however, alone had begun to feel too damn much like lonely.

The city had gone dark except for the streetlamps, and a few lighted offices and the large red letters atop the Chubb Building far to his left. He couldn't see the clouds, but he could feel them, waiting. An automobile passed, tires sounding wet on the tarmac; it was the only one he could see in any direction. Chattanooga was not, he realized, a city whose downtown held much life beyond ordinary business hours, despite the obvious attempts at urban revitalization.

"When's your next shift?" he asked as they walked toward the hotel, several blocks away.

"Don't have one. I'm on administrative leave."

He frowned. "Meaning?"

He felt her stiffen slightly. "Meaning, until I.A. finishes their investigation." She glanced up at him. "That's Internal Affairs."

It was his turn to stiffen, but she tugged lightly on his arm, waving her free hand vaguely toward the street.

"It's all right, they're not following me, it's nothing like that. Corruption or anything, I mean." A deep breath that exhaled quietly. The grip on his arm didn't change. "There was a shooting over at East Bridge last weekend—that's a mall, by the way—and I was involved. A daylight robbery attempt. The guy's dead." She hesitated. "I was the shooter."

He heard no remorse in her tone, nor did he sense any.

"The trouble is, he was black, and I'm not."

"So . . ."

"So it was either desk duty and a whole bunch of stupid papers, or leave until everything's sorted out and the protests calm down a bit. I took the leave."

They were the only ones on the street.

No cars, no buses; it might as well have been midnight.

A faint mist began to fall, and it felt as if they were walking through fog.

Another block, and there were curbside trees, their branches bare, skeleton shadows cast across the damp pavement. Treed islands in the center of the street as well, now, and in the distance the faint sound of an ambulance wailing.

"Here's the thing," she said, fumbling in her purse with her left hand. "Check those reports out tonight. I assume you'll know what you're reading."

"Pretty much," he answered, taking a business card from her. On the back she had written what he gathered was her home telephone number.

"I'll meet you tomorrow for breakfast," she continued. "If you have any questions, ask them then. Then . . . whatever you need me for."

"We can't talk tonight?"

"Is there a rush?"

The last killing had been a fortnight ago, according to the sketchy information Chesney had given him. Anything fresh would have been gone days ago.

He shook his head.

"Good. Because I have a date, and I'll be damned if I'm going to stand him up."

The Read House was on the corner, a narrow canopy stretching from its brick front to the curb. There was no doorman, only a trio of empty newspaper machines. Long windows stretched left and right away from the glass-door entrance—to the right, they displayed clothing for the half-dozen expensive shops inside; to the left he could see small restaurant/bar tables, empty of patrons, in a section cut off from the rest of the room by a latticework wall.

Across the boulevard someone laughed drunkenly, and someone scolded.

They stood for a moment beneath the canopy, backs to a sudden wind, before she released his arm and looked up at him, one eye partially closed. Examining him, the ghost of a smile at her lips .

She wants to ask, he thought, but she probably won't. Not tonight.

"Nine o'clock," she said abruptly, turned, and walked across the street without checking for traffic, toward a large and largely empty parking lot on the opposite corner. He watched until she let herself into a small sedan and drove away. Then he went inside, took the elevator to his floor, and stood for a second in front of his door, searching his pockets for the electronic key.

He hated those things.

They didn't seem real, just stiff cardboard with holes punched in them.

When he found it, he let himself in, softly kicked the door closed behind him, and flicked the wall switch on as he shrugged off his coat. A table lamp was the only illumination, but he didn't need anymore.

One look told him someone had been here while he'd been gone.

It wasn't the maid.

The room had been searched.

10

The room had once been two, the center of the connecting wall replaced by an archway that accentuated the high plaster ceiling and pale floral wallpaper. Opposite the door was a three-cushion couch fronted by a glass-top cocktail table and flanked by end tables on which stood two tall brass lamps; a high window behind the couch overlooked Broad Street, hidden now by thick drapes. To the right was a closet and an inset wet bar backed by a mirror; to his left, a cherry-wood table with three matching padded chairs set around it.

Richard dropped the coat onto the nearest chair and moved toward the arch.

Beyond was a king-size bed with two low nightstands, a window behind it. Facing the footboard was a tall cabinet of scrolled walnut—behind its upper doors was a television, with three drawers set below it. In the far wall was another closet, and the bathroom door.

The sitting-room lamp didn't quite reach that far; all he could see was the near side of the bed. The rest were shapes and shadows.

And a scent.

Before he had left the hotel for the park, he had made sure he'd spoken to the maid who had cleaned his room, a flimsy excuse about misplacing an important paper. They hadn't chatted long, but it was long enough for him to learn her scent.

This wasn't it.

His left hand closed into a loose fist.

He swallowed several times and tightened his jaw to keep his temper from overriding his good sense.

It was a struggle he wasn't so sure he wanted to win.

What he wanted to do was let the Garou take him, take the form and let him rip the place apart; what he had to do was find the one who had invaded his place. And that sparked his anger further, because he knew he wouldn't be able to do it here. As he prowled, nostrils flared, gaze searching slowly, he realized that whoever it had been, had been extraordinarily careful.

Nothing had been disturbed except a drawer not quite closed all the way, a pen not quite in the same position beside the bed's telephone.

He growled quietly.

Scent on his clothes in the drawer, scent on his clothes in the bedroom closet.

His left hand tightened.

Scent in the bathroom.

It hadn't been the cop, the woman. Although she hadn't worn perfume, he could still recall the clear scent of her shower-fresh and warm despite the winter air. He would know it anywhere. And this wasn't it.

When he returned to the sitting room, he switched off the lamp and forced himself to sit on the couch, his eyes narrowed, his breathing deliberately slow.

This wasn't the work of the Warders; they knew better.

It couldn't have been the rogue, because it—he or she—didn't, couldn't, know he was here. Neither would it have been so cautious.

His lungs filled and emptied.

Muted voices in the corridor rose and faded.

The dark took on weight and made his lungs work harder.

Somebody else knew, and his frustration grew when he couldn't focus his concentration on anything but the invading scent that threatened to overwhelm him.

Out, he decided then; he had to get out.

Five minutes later he was on the deserted street behind the hotel, the air much colder, moisture on the tarmac slowly turning to wafer ice. He crossed over and walked on, more rapidly now, lights from a motel across the way blurred as the mist thickened into a light rain.

His shadow kept him company.

A few cars passed, none of them slowing down.

Faster still, nearly running, as he made his way under the interstate overpass, listening to the traffic above him fleeing to the suburbs here and in Georgia, not five minutes away.

Eventually, the land rose to a low, shapeless hill on his right, a few houses at its base, nothing but trees above that he could see.

Faster, trotting, ignoring the rain, the slippery pavement, swerving abruptly into a narrow street without illumination save from a porch-light or two.

His shadow changed.

There was no agony in the transformation, and at his level, no need to discard his clothing.

What he wore merged; what he was, was human no more, although it still ran on two legs.

A dog howled hysterically.

A door slammed.

He ducked into a wooded lot and let his new vision take him through to the hillside, into the trees and up, the rain comfortably cool on black-and-silver fur, the wind taking the scent of him away from the now-invisible houses.

But not away from the creatures whose territory he passed through—dark things stirred and froze at his passing, or bolted from beneath the brush; nesting birds called out softly, a few taking wing, most simply trembling; a rabbit darted across a small clearing, zigzagging, soundless.

It wasn't fast enough.

In a lunging stride, the Strider caught it, and its fangs gleamed wetly despite the dark as they tore into the creature's neck.

Soundless.

Except for the faint raindrop splash of blood on the ground's dead leaves.

Farther up and farther west he caught another, ate, drank, and settled easily on his haunches, bobbing his great head as he tested the air. He was alone. Except for a few nervous birds nearby, he could sense no warm blood, and his hunger subsided, the bloodlust stirred by his temper finally gone. Or at least satisfied for the moment.

Slowly he rose to his full height, grunted, and made his way to the top of the hill. A small clearing sat just below the crown, an irregular oval charred by a summer fire. It was on the back slope, giving him a fairly unobstructed view of the land beyond the city, at least in this direction. It surprised him to see no more than a handful of lights below. Although most of the trees appeared to be pine, he could see, now, how isolated Chattanooga really was in spite of its urban sprawl.

If the rogue he was after was native to the area, finding it was going to be much more difficult than he'd imagined. Too many hills, too many mountains, too much untended, uninhabited woodland.

He turned away, flexed his legs, and began to run again, easily this time, lopping up to the crown and down the other side, branches slapping lightly against his shoulders and sides, at one point slipping on the increasingly slippery ground and nearly falling.

A quick laugh at himself as he regained his balance, exhilarating in the freedom he felt.

He ran for the joy of it until he felt his limbs tiring, and made his way slowly back to level ground.

Shifting on the way.

Thinking about the rogue and relishing the challenge.

Whatever side issues there were, no matter what the Warders had said, the hunt would be for the rogue—everything else would have to wait.

He grinned; he laughed aloud; he felt better than he had in months, and only vaguely noticed the increased activity at the Read House as he made his way quickly to his room. Once there, he changed into dry clothes—dark shirt and jeans, leaving his feet bare—and sat at the table, Chesney's envelope and Minster's folder spread before him.

He knew what would be in the Warder's package—instructions to take care, do not bring attention to yourself, do not (this time) kill the rogue if you can help it, be as swift and silent as you can. There would also be money to take care of his incidentals; the room and its charges would be taken care of by the company he supposedly worked for.

He was in too good a humor to have to read what he already knew.

He opened the folder instead, ignoring the fading scent of the room's intruder. By morning it would be gone, but he wouldn't forget it.

Two hours later he slumped back and rubbed his eyes with the backs of his hands.

"Damn," he whispered.

From the newspaper clippings the detective had also included, he saw that most of the details in these reports hadn't made it into the media, otherwise the story would have made the national news. The last death, Trish McCormick's, was still a front-page topic, however, partly because of the woman's evident beauty, and partly because it had happened only last week. What the clippings didn't tell their readers was how the bodies were when they were discovered.

"Mauled" was too mild a term.

"Partially consumed" was the M.E.'s verdict, something Richard would have guessed anyway.

The second victim had been found in the river, snagged in the branches of a fallen tree only a few hundred yards north of the aquarium; what was left of the third had been found stuffed in a Dumpster out of the valley, behind an upscale mall north of the city.

The first victim, Kyle Gellman, had only been attacked. Richard assumed the reason no feeding had taken place was because the man had been found too soon.

From what he could see, the police investigation had changed its focus from a possible human maniac to the more likely solution of some kind of animal, possibly a panther drifted up from Florida, once the second victim's condition had been examined. Yet here and there, he could see doubt among the investigating officers assigned to the hastily assembled task force. Cannibalism, apparently, was not being ruled out.

He groaned aloud to release some tension, rubbed his face again, and stood, stretching until he felt that his joints threatened to pop. Bed, he ordered; take some rest, talk to Minster tomorrow and have a look around the mountain where Gellman and McCormick were killed. And probably the second victim, a man, had been as well. He had a feeling the woman found behind the mall was an aberration in the pattern.

The doorknob rattled.

Richard whirled, breath held, until it rattled again.

Two strides took him to the peephole, through which he saw a short man with astoundingly thick, long white hair, glaring at his electronic key. Richard opened the door, and the man jumped back, one hand at his chest.

"Wrong room," Richard said with a polite smile.

The man closed his eyes briefly and sighed. He held up the key and snarled at it. "I hate these things. They never remind you what your number is." He glanced at the door's brass numbers, looked to his left, and shrugged. "Damn, there is it. Sorry to have bothered you."

"No problem," Richard said, aware now of a constant noise in the background. People; lots of people.

The floor was shaped like a capital *I*. His room was at the base, just to the right of the corridor's intersection. The white-haired man's room was at the east end of the base, the only other room on this side, and it had double doors, the sign of a large suite.

Richard frowned as he listened. It was late, it was Thursday, so what was going on?

The man had his door open now, and nudged a suitcase over the threshold with one foot. "You part of the convention?" he asked as he stepped inside.

"Convention?"

The man raised his eyebrows. "You're not, I guess. Odd. They usually try to keep the guests all here in one place." He smiled. "So they can keep track of them, I reckon."

The door began to close.

"Excuse me," Richard said, raising his voice. "What convention?"

"Hope you don't like a good night's sleep," the man said, laughing silently. "By dinnertime tomorrow, there'll be a couple of thousand of them crawling all over the place. They take over the whole building until Sunday. Noisy as hell, too. I love it."

The door closed.

Richard stared for a moment before backing into his room. He turned over the bolt, set the chain latch, and scratched idly at his cheek as he headed for the bedroom.

A convention.

Two thousand people.

His first reaction was to swear at Chesney for being such a fool; his second was a slow, careful smile.

Although there would undoubtedly be some inconvenience, this could very well work to his advantage: it was easier to disappear in a crowd of businessmen and their wives, than in a mostly empty building.

Besides, how bad could it be?

11

The temperature rose, but the rain didn't stop. It fell steadily on the back of a slow-moving wind, easing every so often to a drizzle, and every so often strengthening to a downpour that turned the traffic to a blur and sent pedestrians scurrying for the nearest doorway. Mist rose like steam from the gutters. Gusts slammed under the restaurant's awnings and caused the large windows that made up most of its south wall to shimmy.

The glass was cold when Richard touched it with a finger.

He sat alone in a booth, watching the entrance, waiting for Joanne Minster, a cup of coffee cradled between his palms. She had called his room shortly after nine, apologizing that department business would keep her away until noon, perhaps a little later. Although he was anxious to get started, he hadn't really minded when he checked outside and saw that the weather had gotten worse. There would be no spoors to pick up, not the way things were now.

On the other hand, that meant one more day for the rogue to remain free.

He had used the extra time to go over the reports once more, and the more he read, the more he wondered exactly what he was missing. Ordinarily, a rogue was increasingly affected by his madness. His movement patterns became erratic, his attacks more bold and vicious, and he seldom bothered to try to hide his tracks.

And the freefall into madness seldom took more than a couple of months.

This one was different.

Once a month since late October, give or take a few days, someone had died.

There was no telling whether or not any of the victims had been stalked; none of the interviews with family and friends indicated it, but that didn't mean much. Rogue or not, Garou weren't that careless when it came to the hunt.

And as far as the police were concerned, there were no useable tracks, either animal or human.

He wished he could talk to Fay. She had always been able to cut through the inconsequential details without batting an eye, steering him away from the irrelevant details that threatened to clutter up his mind. He knew he would get there sooner or later; Fay had the knack of making it sooner.

He had already tried calling half a dozen times, but hadn't been able to reach her. Concern made him call another number which routed through several area codes until he was able to speak to someone who could give a message to John Chesney. Every other time he had taken this step, the Warder had gotten back to him within the hour.

Chesney didn't call, and he didn't like the sudden feeling that he had been thrust into the dark, and no one had any intention of giving him some light.

Jesus, he thought then, and squeezed his eyes

shut, deliberately tightly enough to spark mild pain.
Jesus, do you think you could get a little more melodramatic, you idiot?

He shook his head slightly and glanced outside,
wincing in sympathy when he saw a woman racing
down the street after her umbrella. By the time she
reached it, he thought, she might as well not bother.

Another check of the entrance made him look at
his watch; it was just past one, and no sign yet of the
detective.

What he did see was a steady parade of people he
imagined were checking in for this convention. They
didn't, however, appear to business types at all.
Most seemed to be young, almost all in clothes that
ran from the carefully casual to the outright grungy.
Suitcases and backpacks bulged, bellmen's carts
were loaded with cartons and packages, and almost
all of them appeared to know everyone else.

The restaurant began to fill.

It was a long, pleasant room, with booths along
the window wall, tables everywhere else. A small bar
carved its own niche midway toward the back, and
beyond it he could see a pair of chefs working over a
steaming grill. Two waitresses and a waiter floated
around the tables, sidestepping boisterous reunions
with an ease and unconcern that made him suspect
they had been through all this many times before.
One of them stopped by to refill his cup, but slipped
away before he could ask any questions.

Several times couples or groups drifted past, staring pointedly, clearly hoping he would take the
hint—a single man taking up a large booth, while
they had to scrounge for an extra chair for a smaller
table.

Finally, one man, in a rumpled safari jacket and
stone-washed jeans, with a gray-shot beard that

should have been trimmed six months ago, stood over him, glaring, until he looked up.

"Yes?" he said mildly.

The man didn't answer, just an irritated wave toward the empty seat.

"I'm expecting someone," Richard explained, still smiling.

Again the man didn't answer; his frown did it for him, and Richard had had enough. He picked up his cup, glanced out the window, looked back at the man and stared.

Just . . . stared.

. . . *green fire* . . .

The man blinked in confusion several times, opened his mouth, and hastily backed away. When he tried to stammer an apology, Richard deliberately turned his head toward the window, feeling the momentary fear and confusion, and scolding himself. The man had done nothing but be a little rude; he didn't deserve the fright.

Voices were raised, laughter at the weather which, he gathered, seemed to be a running joke around here this time of year.

A minute later the restaurant fell abruptly silent, one of those curious moments when all conversation halted for no particular reason.

He looked at the street and realized that the wind and rain had finally stopped, but the sky had darkened. Before he could take a breath, an enormous peal of thunder exploded over the hotel, rattling the panes, making everyone jump. The lights flickered, died, and came on again.

A heartbeat more of silence, then everyone began to talk at once, nervously and nervously laughing. Somewhere behind him, in a small area in front set off by a latticework-and-glass wall, a baby cried.

"That'll get the blood running," said Joanne Minster, sliding into the booth opposite him.

Richard started, and she grinned as she yanked a scarf from her head and fluffed at her damp hair. She wore a fleece-lined denim jacket over a baggy rust sweater, and a tiny gold ankh hung from a fine gold chain around her neck.

"You eat yet?"

He nodded at his cup. "Just coffee."

"Good. I'm starving." She twisted around to get a waitress' attention, turned back when she did, and said, "Sorry I'm late. Department stuff, like I said. It's a pain in the butt, but I don't have a lot to say about my life these days."

He said nothing until after the waitress, polite but harried, had taken their lunch order. "I want to talk to that girl. Polly Logan."

Joanne lifted a sculpted eyebrow. "You sure? I mean, that was months ago." She grabbed a small notepad from a black shoulder bag, flipped it open, and thumbed through the pages. "Seems to me that Hendean guy, Leon, at the hang-gliding place, would be better. It was only last week, you know?"

"He didn't see anything," Richard reminded her.

"Neither did the girl."

"Maybe."

He could tell she was unsettled, and it wasn't the weather. Long fingers darted over her food when it arrived, and she tried not to stare at him when she thought he wasn't looking. Department stuff, he thought; sure, right. She had probably spent the morning trying to find out if he was who she'd been told he was.

She hadn't learned a thing, and that must have raised a red flag or two.

Then she pointed at his plate, at the barely brown

chopped sirloin, nothing else, not even greens. "You really ought to try cooked food now and then. What the hell are you going to get from that?"

"Nourishment," he answered dryly.

She laughed. "Why don't you just eat it raw?"

"Too hard to catch."

She laughed again, silently this time, and he decided there was a very good chance he could grow to like this woman. She was clearly suspicious of him, or of what he appeared to represent, but that didn't seem to get in the way of what had to be done. She was no doubt convinced she would figure it out before long. With or without his help.

Besides, if he was going to be honest, aside from her obvious intelligence, she wasn't all that hard on the eyes, either.

He grinned to himself then, quickly bent his head so the grin wouldn't show, thinking that a remark like that wouldn't earn him any points with a woman like her.

As he ate, she explained that her orders were simple: she was to assist him in any way possible, smooth things over with bruised egos who might think he was trying to steal thunder and credit, and make sure he didn't step on too many toes. "A snap," she said wryly. "I can do it in my sleep."

Not once did she ask for an explanation of his presence. By her tone, she obviously believed he would perform the courtesy without having to be prodded.

Then she waved a fork at the room and filled him in on the purpose of the convention: writers and readers of science fiction and fantasy from all over the South, she told him, with a sprinkling from other parts of the country. They filled the place to capacity once a year, listened to panels, watched movies, spent tons of money here and elsewhere in town, wore funny clothes at night, got drunk, got laid, and went home Sunday afternoon.

The police were usually around, but there was seldom any trouble. The convention had its own security, and handled its own problems pretty well.

This year, evidently, the emphasis was going to be on costumes, so he shouldn't be surprised to see TV and movie characters walking around all day.

"You wouldn't know it to look at them," she said, "but most of them, the rest of the year, actually have a life."

"More power to them," he muttered, and signaled for the check.

"Hey," she said, "did I say something wrong?"

He shook his head as he stood. But the afternoon had grown noticeably brighter while they'd had their lunch, and he didn't want to waste any more time. As long as these people didn't get in his way, he really didn't care what they did or what they wore.

Frowning at his change of mood, she took him to the front entrance, where her car waited in a no parking zone. "Privilege," she explained blithely, sliding in behind the wheel, and took off before he was settled.

They headed south, away from the hotel, not speaking until the city's center had been replaced by low, whitewashed warehouses, bars, and a handful of restaurants with garish neon signs that at night probably looked inviting, but in daylight it only underscored their drab exteriors.

A mile or so later, she pulled sharply into the nearly deserted parking lot of a large supermarket, and stopped without cutting the engine. There were three other cars, a few forlorn shopping carts, and scraps and pages of newspaper fluttering wetly on the tarmac. Lookout Mountain rose starkly, sharply, directly ahead. Bare trees exposed a handful of small houses on the lower slope, and the color of pine only added to the bleak northern face.

The top was hidden in clouds.

Richard leaned forward and looked up to where the slope abruptly became vertical. "People live up there?"

"Nice town," she answered defensively. "Only the tourists make noise." She nodded at the mountain. "It isn't fat, but it stretches back a ways. McCormick, last week, was found around there, to the right. You can't see it from here. It's a couple of miles along."

Without warning, she pulled out of the lot. A block later the road forked beneath a hanging traffic light. "The back way," she told him, pointing to the right. "We're going up the easy way."

Five minutes after the announcement, he doubted there even was an easy way up.

The road was narrow and steep, winding sharply around the contours of the slope, and she took it at speed. On the right a steep bank, wooded, with a glimpse of an occasional house or garage; on the left, a low guard rail that wouldn't, he thought grimly, stop a scooter from breaking through and plummeting to the bottom. They were only halfway up, and already he didn't like how small the buildings down there looked.

"Heights get to you?" she asked, taking a right-hand curve easily, and too fast.

He shook his head. "Nope. Can't fly, that's all."

"Life's too short," was all she said as the curve veered left around an outcropping of bare rock.

There had been no other traffic since they had left the city behind. The few homes he could see were dark, more than a few were boarded up. A bulge of thin fog left the woods here and there, and a constant drizzle kept the road gleaming.

Another huge boulder swung them left again, and for a second all he could see was the valley between the boles of spindly trees.

Then Joanne said, "Oh, shit."

The pickup was black, its windshield tinted too dark to show the driver.

It moved slowly, but it was in the wrong lane.

Richard braced one hand on the dashboard as Joanne hit the horn, then touched the brakes and yanked on the wheel to take them into the outside lane.

Without any hesitation, the pickup swerved over at the same time, glancing off the guard rail before centering on the lane.

"Jesus!" she yelled, braked and yanked the wheel again, but this time the tires finally lost their traction.

12

Richard watched helplessly as the world spun by in terrifying slow motion—trees, sky, trees again, the grinning grill of the pickup, and finally the pocked face of the boulder as Joanne, somehow, used the car's skid to take them onto the narrow verge on the right where they jounced over a spindly bush before shuddering to a halt, not two feet shy of a thick-bored pine.

The truck didn't stop.

For a long time nothing moved, and the only sound was the slow ticking of cooling metal.

Then Joanne slammed herself back in her seat and punched the steering wheel twice, and twice again. "Son of a bitch." A snarl, and she kicked open the door, jumped out and screamed, "Son of a god-damn bitch!" at the empty road. She stamped a foot on the tarmac, kicked viciously at a pebble, and spun in a tight circle, punching the air with her left hand before, red-faced and panting, she leaned over and looked in the car. "You okay?"

He turned his head slowly. "I told you . . . I can't fly."

"Bastard," she muttered, glaring down the mountain. "Goddamn blind bastard."

Richard opened his own door and, after a moment's pause to be sure he wouldn't fall, made his way around the rear bumper and through what was left of the bush, his legs trembling slightly, his vision preternaturally clear. The drizzle felt good on his face, and he closed his eyes briefly and licked his suddenly dry lips. His stomach lurched once; a chill touched the back of his neck.

For him, for his kind, dying wasn't easy, but once over that guard rail, it would have been.

He looked at Joanne and shook his head in admiration. "You are one hell of a driver, Detective."

With a vague it-was-nothing gesture she sagged abruptly against the front fender. "Tell you the truth, I don't feel like it right now." A steady hand passed over her face and back through her hair. "But thanks."

He squinted against a sudden, damp breeze and hunched his shoulders. There were highlights in the valley as sunlight broke through small gaps in the scudding clouds. Another hour, he thought, and there'd be no trace of the storm.

He cleared his throat; it felt packed with cotton. "Could you see him?"

"The driver?" She narrowed her eyes in concentration. "No. Probably some old fart, or some drunk." She spat dryly. "Stupid bastard."

He walked around the jut of the boulder, using the damp stone to keep his balance; the road was empty, and he could hear no engine either approaching or fading. When he returned, she was on the edge of the front seat, hands draped over her knees, staring at the road.

He stood in front of her, waiting until she looked

up. "Bastard, yes," he told her. "Stupid, no." He jerked a thumb toward the spot where he had first seen the truck. "He was waiting there for us, Jo. When we came around the bend, he didn't move until he was sure."

She looked at him in confusion, grabbed the top of the door and hauled herself to her feet. "Are you sure?"

He walked over to the guard rail where the truck had ricocheted off, heard her follow as he crouched and pushed at the dirt and leaves beneath it.

"What?"

"Damn," he whispered, and straightened, holding up a jagged square of glass. "I saw something as we came up, but it happened too fast." He dropped it into her open palm. "It's not a headlight, it's part of a mirror. He could see us coming, but we couldn't see him."

"From up there?" She looked doubtful.

"It doesn't take much. Just enough to know we were what he wanted." He sniffed, and wiped his mouth with the back of his hand. "When he hit the rail, it was no accident. He wanted that mirror gone."

She bounced the shard thoughtfully in her hand, then tucked it into her jeans pocket. A nod got them back into the car, and after a deep breath, she turned on the engine, took another deep breath, and pulled out onto the road.

"What you're saying is, he had to know we were coming," she said quietly.

He nodded.

"He must have been . . . he was in the restaurant."

"Or an accomplice, yes, someone to phone ahead and let this guy know where we would be."

She drove in silence for the next few minutes, flinching when a line of cars rounded a curve ahead of them, glancing in the rearview mirror until they were well out of sight. Richard, meanwhile, stared out his window, seeing nothing but drab colors, no shapes at all.

It could be a trap, the Warders had told him; it was possible someone wanted to put him out of business.

"Possible" was no longer the operative word.

"You know," she said at last, "you haven't been in town all that long. And if nobody knows who you are or why you're here, who the hell did you piss off?"

He couldn't answer because he didn't know.

A final turn, the land flattened, and they were there, in Lookout Mountain. Mostly white houses, most of them clapboard, a few brick and stone; hedges and picket fences, all of it looking a little old, a little weary under the clouds that hung not far above the trees. Here there was still no sunlight.

"The park," he said suddenly. "Take me to this park, then get the girl and bring her."

The car slowed.

"You going to tell me why?"

He heard the anger, and he ignored it. "No."

Her voice was taut, without emotion: "Whatever you say, you're the boss."

If I live that long, he thought.

The lobby of the Read House was two-stories high. Thick, dark, wood pillars rose from an expansive Oriental-style carpet to a gallery above. Around the carpet's perimeter were settings of high-backed chairs and love seats, cocktail tables and end tables. A small glass-door entrance was recessed in the south wall, facing across the lobby an elegant, now-closed restaurant. The west wall held the long registration counter, crowded now with lines of conventioneers checking in; a portion of the east wall was taken up by a pair of brass-door elevators.

One of them opened, and Miles Blanchard stepped out.

He glanced around as if trying to orientate himself, then headed directly for the nearest vacant chair. He sat with a sigh and a smile, lit a cigarette with a wood match, and dropped the match into an already-filled ash tray on the table beside him. He crossed his legs, leaned back, and blew a perfect smoke ring toward the vaulted ceiling.

Although he wore a dark, pinstripe suit with a muted red club tie, he didn't feel at all out of place. These people were here to have fun, maybe do a little business, and that, he figured, was exactly his own purpose.

The only annoyance had been his room.

The hotel was divided into two sections—this, the original nineteenth-century building, and a newer addition beside it, on the other side of the mostly underground parking garage. To get there, he had to go to the fifth floor and use a skywalk to cross over the garage roof. The inconvenience was minor, however. Soon enough he'd figure out another way to enter and leave without being seen.

He already knew which room was Richard Turpin's.

Besides, these people were fascinating. Had he not been on assignment, he might well have taken the weekend just to hang around and observe them.

As it was, on impulse, he had registered himself as a member, the easier to move among the growing crowds without having to answer questions.

The suit, however, would have to go eventually. Costumes were apparently going to be the order of the day once the convention began, and he had already been mistaken for one of the featured guests listed in a program he had been handed when he had signed up, and he didn't want the attention, no matter how flattering it had been. He didn't want to have to use his kit more than absolutely necessary.

In fact, he rather enjoyed the face he had chosen today—shading to make it lean, graying brown hair, sideburns, mustache, a blunted goatee that, he decided when he studied his reflection, gave him a subtle, rakish look. Pirate, perhaps, or the Sheriff of Nottingham.

Movement on his left turned his head slowly.

A thirty-ish woman took the wingback chair on the other side of the table. Slender, fair skin, high forehead, her cheeks lightly flushed and dusted lightly with freckles. She wore a fawn topcoat opened to expose a dark, silklike blouse and matching slacks. From a bulging pouch at her waist she took a leather cigarette case, took one out and put it to her lips.

Blanchard struck a match, leaned over, and lit the cigarette for her.

She inhaled, blew the smoke out in a rush, and touched a finger to her lips.

"Well?" he asked pleasantly.

She shrugged as she studied the tip of the cigarette. "If he's not dead, which he probably isn't, he's going to be looking behind him all the time from now on."

"Oh, I do hope he's not dead," he said with mock solemnity. "It would spoil the whole party."

Her laugh was more a grunt.

He sighed his satisfaction—the game had well begun—and grinned. "Love your hair."

Wanda Strand scowled her disgust. "Oh, please." It was shoulder-length, fair and fine, and at the moment damp and frizzy. "If it rains anymore, it'll look like I'm wearing a goddamn helmet."

Blanchard crossed his legs. "Where is he now?"

"Talking to the girl, most likely. If he can get by that old dragon who watches her."

He nodded. "He can. But he won't learn anything."

"Are you positive?"

"What does it matter even if he does?" He blew another smoke ring, and a passing young woman applauded sarcastically. He nodded pleasantly to her and, when she was gone, lowered his voice. "Even with that cop around, he won't live long enough to tell anyone anyway."

The woman didn't answer.

She didn't have to.

The pillars climbed past the gallery to a vaulted ceiling, and between them arches of polished paneled wood framed small areas where chairs and tables had been set against low railings with filigree below.

The rogue sat alone, right above hotel registration, and looked down at Blanchard and the woman, finding it almost impossible not to laugh aloud.

They seemed so earnest, so intent, so incredibly goddamn serious, it was nearly farcical. If they could only see themselves down there, children plotting away in the midst of chaos, smoking like steam engines . . . he looking pitifully out of place, and she looking as if she'd rather be anyplace else but here.

It sighed, then placed two fingers to its temples, pressing hard.

The headache was back, subtle and insistent.

Its return was unexpected, and the rogue couldn't help a moment of anxiety as its fingers massaged in small circles, slowly, almost absently, less a cure than a means to pass the time until the throbbing passed.

If it got too bad, there would have to be a hunt whether he wanted it or not.

If there was a hunt, there was a fair chance Richard Turpin would succeed.

Or he would have done, in the past.

But the Strider had never come up against competition like this.

If the stories and rumors were right, the other rogues had been certifiably mad, unable to handle the twin poles of their existence. They had lost touch with Gaia, and with the center of their selves. Killing assuaged the hunger; nothing else mattered, not even the feeding.

Not this time.

The hunger was satisfied, but this time there was an additional goal. When it was achieved, the rogue would never have to worry again.

About anything.

And Richard Turpin would be dead.

13

Joanne stood beside her car and glared at the entrance to the mountain park. She was mad. No, she was furious. At Richard Turpin, for treating her like a rookie who didn't even deserve to know the time of day, and at herself for reacting to him this way. It wasn't as if they were partners. She had no special standing as far as he was concerned.

Yet it was galling nonetheless.

Get the girl. Bring her to me. Fetch, Jo, fetch.

Jesus, she thought; get a grip, you idiot, it's only for a couple of days.

On the other hand, someone had tried to run them off the road, and even now her stomach filled with bile when she saw that pickup deliberately switch lanes.

"Sergeant?"

She blinked herself back and looked over the car's roof at Polly Logan, and couldn't help smiling. The young woman was bundled as if for deepest winter, complete with mittens and a wool cap. Although there had been moments of sunlight, shafts of it teasing the houses, taunting the streets, the cloud cover had thickened again, but the temperature hadn't fallen. Not yet.

Doris Maurin stood protectively behind her, a tall, thin woman of indeterminate age, her thick, black hair without a spot of gray. She wore only a light jacket over a sweater and jeans, her left hand clutching a black purse as if it were a gun.

"This had better be good," the woman said. "It's been months, you know. Months."

Joanne assured her, as she had twice already, that the meeting with Turpin was necessary, and that it wouldn't take very long.

As they walked toward the gray stone towers, Polly in the middle, Mrs. Maurin shook her head. "Government, you say?"

"Yes."

"FBI?"

Joanne didn't answer with more than a noncommittal grunt, because she really didn't know. Two days ago, Lt. Millson had called her into his office and told her she would be spending part of her administrative leave showing a Washington investigator around. Apparently the Feds, for whatever reasons, were interested in their serial killer. She had asked the same question, and the lieutenant had only handed her a strapped folder and said, "For now, Minster, you don't need to know."

There had been no room for argument, and, for a change, she had been wise enough not to start one. She was pleased, however, that at least he hadn't tried to foist off the preposterous story about a marauding wild animal.

Instead, she had spent this morning trying to track Turpin down, to find some trace of him through the department's computer connections to law enforcement agencies across the country. As far as they were concerned, however, the man didn't exist. He was a ghost.

For a ghost, though, he sure had a lot of obviously powerful friends, and she was no longer quite convinced she ought to know more than she did.

Which, she thought bitterly, wasn't a whole hell of a lot.

Polly slowed as they neared the entrance.

Mrs. Maurin immediately put a hand on her arm. "It's all right, dear, nothing to worry about. We're just going to talk, that's all, you don't have to worry."

Joanne felt terrible. The apprehension on Polly's face had turned to fear, and her lower lip began to tremble. "Mrs. Maurin is right, honey," she said gently, a gentle touch on the young woman's shoulder. "There isn't anything here now that's going to hurt you."

Polly nodded uncertainly. "I used to like the park."

Joanne managed a smile.

"I don't anymore."

They stepped through to the other side, and Polly stopped, staring at the ground, hands jammed into her pockets.

"Damn good reason," Mrs. Maurin muttered.

The blacktop path branched in several directions around the small park. Large, leafless trees studded the grassy areas between, and along the divergent paths white-globed lampposts looked like trees themselves. In the center, on a small rise, marble steps led up to a large dome held up by marble pillars, a monument to the Union and Confederate soldiers who fought in the Battle of Chattanooga. The whole park was only a few acres, its perimeter made of trees and shrubs, boulders and iron railings; beyond was the valley in which the city lay, nearly two thousand feet straight down.

"So where is he?" Mrs. Maurin demanded.

A soft wind began to sift through the bare branches, and a handful of dead leaves scuttled across the brown grass.

Joanne looked around before pointing straight ahead. "There."

Turpin walked toward them from the far end, taking the easily sloping ground slowly, face up to the wind; almost, she realized, as if he were sniffing it, testing it for a sign.

The three women walked toward him, Polly no longer lagging.

"Oh, my," Mrs. Maurin whispered. "Oh, my, honey, if he's not yours, I want him."

Joanne grinned, but said nothing. She was struck again by how almost ordinary he seemed. Not tall, not hefty, the silver-touched brown hair neither giving nor taking age. Almost ordinary. Except for those eyes, the slight slant of them and the dark green of them.

Mrs. Maurin fanned herself with one hand. "My, my, my."

Polly giggled. "Miss Doris, behave yourself."

Joanne relaxed. The girl seemed to be all right now, her expression bright as Richard smiled at her, holding out his hand as he approached. Polly took it and blushed, her gaze skittering away when he told her, quietly, to please call him Richard.

"I don't want you to be afraid," he said gently, glancing at Joanne.

"I'm not," Polly said shyly. "Not now."

Another glance, this one an order, and Joanne tilted her head at Mrs. Maurin, taking them a few yards away, out of earshot. It bothered her that she wouldn't be able to eavesdrop on the interrogation, but she also recognized that her presence might prevent Polly from saying what Richard needed to know.

Mrs. Maurin lit a cigarette once they stopped beneath the nearest tree, blew smoke into the wind, and batted it away before it stung her eyes. "He's wasting his time, dear. Polly hasn't said a word about that night since it happened."

Joanne shrugged; it wasn't her call. "How . . . I mean, Polly, is she. . . ?"

Mrs. Maurin smiled. "How bad is she, is that what you want to know?" Another puff, this time over her shoulder. "She's not the best of my babies, no getting around that, but she'll be all right given a little more time. She's twenty-five, poor child, be twenty-six come April, but she'll always be no more than thirteen or fourteen. If that." Her voice grew melancholy. "Not a bad age to be, when you think about it."

"Will she be able to live on her own?"

"Oh, sure, dear. It just takes time, that's all. And that's what I've plenty of." She laughed through a cloud of smoke. "That, and a whole ton of patience."

Joanne looked over without being obvious about it—Polly was animated, hands gesturing, eyes wide, while Richard nodded as if every word she said was more important to him than anything else he could think of.

Well, she thought grudgingly, he's damn good, I have to give him that.

Still, she couldn't help checking the park entrance, half expecting to see that black pickup roar between the turrets. She shuddered and hugged herself, rubbing her arms briefly, looking at the sky and the strips of swirling gray that escaped from the black.

"So, honey," said Mrs. Maurin, crushing the cigarette out beneath her sole, "you got a man or what?"

"He was hurt," said Polly sadly.

"I know," Richard answered.

"He scared me."

He nodded. "I know. I can tell."
"Your eyes are different."
Richard smiled. "I know."

The wind began to keen.

The clouds lowered.

A twig snapped off a leaning, twisted tree and flew like a dart until it shattered against the monument steps.

Two couples wandered into the park, looked around and made their disappointment clear by the hunch of their shoulders as they left again, without a sound.

The wind died.

The air began to haze, and outlines softened while the city disappeared.

There was no sound at all but the bell-like sound of Polly's laughter.

Joanne leaned back against a trunk and folded her arms across her chest. Her admiration for Richard's rapport with the girl had soured into annoyance. She was damp, she was cold, and she couldn't understand what Polly could say that would take them so long. It had been in the middle of the night, for God's sake.

What the hell could she have seen? What the hell could she say that she hadn't already told the police?

She made a soft noise of disgust and watched as Mrs. Maurin lit yet another cigarette, seemingly unconcerned, filling the time with a nonstop monologue about the other girls—there were four—who lived at the halfway house. By her tone, however, there was no mistaking the fact that Polly, to her, was special.

And it didn't seem to matter that Joanne wasn't really listening.

*   *   *

"It was scary when he tried to grab me."

"I'll bet it was."

Polly scratched behind her ear. "There were noises, too, you know."

"Well, he'd been hit, Polly. He was hurting."

"No." She shook her head emphatically. "No, not him. The other one."

A vehicle pulled up at the entrance, its headlights high and glaring. Joanne pushed away from the tree, trying to see past them to whatever lay beyond.

"Fool idiot," Mrs. Maurin grumbled, shading her eyes with one hand. "It ain't that foggy out."

But it was, Joanne thought nervously; it was foggy enough that she could barely see the tops of the turrets, and they were only about fifty yards away. And foggy enough that the headlights smeared her vision, gave her nothing to focus on until she looked away.

The older woman edged closer.

"Mrs. Maurin," Joanne said, suddenly remembering the house, "in your front hall there, I saw some bulletin boards by the door and the staircase."

"Yes. We keep track of who's going where, and when. Everybody has to sign in or out." A rueful smile. "At least that's the theory."

"No, I saw those. I mean farther back, by the stairs."

"Oh!" The woman nodded. "The girls call it the Pride Board. You know, when they make something nice to hang up, or when they get a nice letter, things like that."

"Pictures?"

"I don't have a camera."

The headlights didn't leave.

"Drawings, I mean."

"Why sure. There's Charlie Wills, she's a cute little thing, not much good for anything else, but she sure can use a brush. I got the aquarium people to take some small things on consignment last summer for that gift shop they have. Sold them, too. She'll never be a Rembrandt, but I think she'll make enough some day so she can . . ." She paused and looked up, shook her head. "Move out, I was going to say." She looked at Joanne sideways. "I hate when they do that, you know. I know it's my job, but I just hate it."

"What about Polly? Does she draw?"

"All the time, poor thing, all the time."

Richard watched the girl's eyes, deer's eyes caught in a wood, being hunted. He said nothing; he didn't dare.

Finally, she cleared her throat and gave him a false smile. "I don't know. I mean, Mr. Abbott, he's got this little bitty dog, it looks like silly rat when it's wet, but it wasn't like that. You know? It wasn't like that."

"It's okay, Polly. I know what you mean."

Wide-eyed, she looked up. "No," she said. "Oh no, you don't know at all."

Joanne clamped down her excitement. "Where are—"

"Hush." Mrs. Maurin held up a finger and looked over Joanne's shoulder. "Well, damn, she's gone now."

Joanne turned around, and saw the girl shifting her weight from foot to foot, bobbing her head, shaking it, bobbing it again.

"Damn."

Mrs. Maurin lifted her chin. "Polly? Girl? You come on over here, now, you hear? Time we were getting back to the house." Then she lowered her voice. "I'm sorry, Sergeant, but when she gets that way, she's gone for hours. Sometimes days."

Angrily, she flicked a cigarette into the fog. "Took me a month to bring her back after . . . that killing."

The headlights hadn't moved.

Joanne waited until the girl started over, said, "Don't go anywhere just yet," and marched up the path toward the light. She kept her head up and her arms swinging, trying to appear as official as she could, given the clothes she wore. Whoever it was, she swore, he was going get his ass royally chewed.

She heard the engine then, soft and throbbing.

The headlights backed away.

She didn't slow down, she didn't speed up.

Stupid son of a bitch, she thought, able to see now the vague outline of a car; play games with me, you son of a bitch, you're gonna find your ass in a cell. Stupid bastard.

The engine gunned, and she hesitated before realizing the car wasn't going to charge her. It turned a fast circle instead and sped away, taillights dimming quickly, until there was nothing left but the engine. Mocking her as it faded.

She stopped ten feet from the gateway, rolled her eyes, and turned around. Polly was already there, Mrs. Maurin's arm around her shoulders.

"It wasn't his fault," the woman said when she saw Joanne's face. "The girl just gets this way sometimes when she's upset, that's all." She hugged the girl before leading her away. "Should have talked in the house. My fault."

Joanne watched helplessly until the fog took them as well, and her anger boiled over. With hands bunched into fists, she whirled to confront Turpin.

He wasn't there.

The lampposts didn't help; their glow was diffused, creating more shadows than light.

"Turpin!"

She stomped toward the monument. If there were spotlights, they weren't on.

"Turpin, damn it, where are you?"

He didn't answer.

What she heard instead was a deep-throated growl.

14

He stepped out from behind a tree and tapped her on the shoulder.

Joanne spun around, right hand reaching for the small of her back as she dropped into a crouch.

Richard held up a quick hand to hold her off and cover his smile. "Hey, wait, wait, it's me."

Her eyes widened, and for a moment he thought she would still pull the revolver he knew she kept back there. It had been a stupid thing, but he hadn't been able to resist it. The timing and the setting had been too perfect.

The hand stayed up, palm out. "Don't say it," he warned, the smile turning to a grin. "Stupid son of a bitch bastard, I know all that already." The hand lowered slowly. "I'm sorry, okay? I'm sorry."

It was a long second before he saw the tension drain, her shoulders relax as she straightened and made a show of dusting her hands on her jeans. "Never again," she said, walking past him, not looking up. "Never."

He agreed, apologized again, but couldn't get rid of the smile. It wasn't so much the easy trick as it was the information Polly had given him. Eyes, she had said; terrible eyes. Until he eased it out of her, she hadn't really been sure she'd actually seen them. She said something about seeing lights in the sky that no one believed, and so had doubted the eyes and had kept that to herself.

Eyes.

Terrible eyes.

There and gone in an instant, while she had been screaming.

Not green, like his—they had been the pale red of a rogue's advancing madness.

Despite the Warders' insistence, he had needed confirmation for himself. They had been wrong before. Not this time.

Now was the time for hunting.

The next step was to decide how far he could trust Joanne.

As they walked to her car, he wondered how involved she would let herself get in this case. A lot, he figured when she yanked open her door and glared him the order to get in. She didn't seem the type to simply step back, be his faithful liaison, mind her own business.

They sat in silence while she fumed.

If he decided she would truly be a partner, then, she would have to know. It couldn't be avoided. And there was no telling how she would react.

It wasn't an unusual situation; rare, but not unusual. Of those times when his contacts had found out, when he had voluntarily lifted the Veil just for them, only twice had he regretted it. His right hand absently drifted to his left shoulder, pressing lightly in the hollow between shoulder and ribs. The scar had never healed properly.

Unusual, but not rare.

It wasn't the only scar he carried.

Those two—one man, one woman—hadn't lived long enough to lift the Veil for others. He dearly hoped it wouldn't be the same for Joanne.

"Now what?" she asked stiffly.

He considered what he had known and what he knew now, and gestured at the windshield. "That guy, the one who runs the hang-gliding business. Hendean. I want to see that place, and maybe the place where the woman died."

"Now?" She frowned her puzzlement. "There isn't going to be anyone there, not in this weather."

"Maybe there is," he countered softly. "Please. Humor me."

She didn't like it, that much was obvious, but she drove through town without questioning him, taking him along a two-lane road that followed the narrowing crest of the mountain. The houses soon grew sporadic, the only structure of note a large, pale, brick complex on the right, whose sign told him it was Coventry College.

He didn't ask; she didn't volunteer.

The fog thinned quickly, and what remained was swiftly shredded as the wind picked up again, slow and fitful.

They passed occasional houses whose front yards were small, and whose back yards, he thought, must have been mostly straight down. Before long, however, the trees took over, and through the bare branches he could see the spread of land below, and hazy hills in the distance. It was mostly woodland down there, broken only by fields waiting for spring planting.

Joanne cleared her throat. "I told them—Polly and Mrs. Maurin—that you were FBI." A rabbit skittered across the road, and she swerved easily to avoid it. "So what are you? Really?"

"Spooky." He grinned when she glanced over. "Really spooky."

"You got that right," she answered, and he looked away when he saw the start of a smile part her lips.

Better, he thought; it's getting better, thank God. For all his years, all his experience, handling women's moods and tempers was absolutely beyond him.

Fifteen minutes later she pulled onto the gravel skirt outside the Hendean launch area. The barnlike shed was weathered with spotty gray, LEON'S AIR stenciled in red and blue on the sharply canted roof. There were no other cars, no sign of any flyers.

"Waste of time," she muttered as they got out.

Richard walked to the concrete lip and looked down. Straight down. Wishing he hadn't when he felt his stomach lurch and grow as cold as the mountain-top air. God, he thought, swallowing hard; people actually, willingly, throw themselves off here? He shook himself and stepped back, and saw Joanne watching him closely.

"Acrophobia?" she said with just a hint of mocking.

"I don't think so," he answered, heading for the only door he could see. "Like I said, I don't fly."

"You should try it sometime. It's a real rush."

He raised an eyebrow. "You have?"

"Once."

"Only once?"

"Are you kidding, Turpin? I was scared spitless. I think I screamed all the way down. But there's no getting around it, it was a hell of a rush."

The unmarked door was open, and they stepped over the threshold into one vast room. Frames and foils hung from beams overhead, stirring slightly as drafts found cracks in the walls. Around the walls were workbenches, metal tool cabinets, a soda machine, and, just left of the door, a table he figured Hendean used for a desk.

In the center of the smooth concrete floor was a smaller work table, at whose bench sat a man in baggy bib coveralls fussing with a length of aluminum tubing caught in a vice. He was thin, with thinning, curly white hair, and granny glasses that kept slipping down the length of his nose. When he noticed them, he grinned and rose.

"Man," Joanne whispered.

He was tall, very tall, with watery blue eyes and, despite his lean frame, pudgy cheeks. Despite the hair, he wasn't that old. "Hey, hey," he said pleasantly, wiping his hands on a rag. "Closed today, folks."

Joanne nodded and introduced them.

Curly Guestin shook their hands eagerly. "Police, huh? FBI, huh? Wow. I do something wrong?" He laughed, and his face reddened. "Hey, nope. Not me." He gestured toward the table. "I just keep folks from falling out of the sky."

"We're looking for Mr. Hendean," Richard said.

"Gone." Guestin frowned in thought before nodding. "Yep, he's gone. Was here, now he's not. Went down the city, I think. I don't know if he'll be back." He looked at the rafters. "You want to fly?"

"No," said Richard quickly. "No, thanks."

The man dropped abruptly onto the bench, hands clasped between his knees, head bowed. "It's the lady, isn't it. You don't want to fly 'cause the lady got killed."

"No," Joanne said gently. "In fact, that's what we want to talk to Mr. Hendean about. We'd like to know just what happened before she died."

"Wasn't the fall," the man said quickly. "Like I told those police who kept asking me all those questions, same questions over and over, it wasn't me that fixed her gear. Hey, I do good work, y'know?" He looked up at them, his smile painful and brief. "Some kind of maniac out there, FBI," he said solemnly. "Hardly safe around here anymore. Even the regulars aren't making it all the time."

"Then why are you here all by yourself?" Joanne asked.

Guestin grinned, reached under the table, and pulled out a shotgun. "If he comes in here, I'll take his maniac head off." Another laugh, and again his face reddened. As he put the gun back under the table, he told them he didn't expect his boss back until morning. There was, he explained, lots to do, making sure the people came back after what he called "the accident." Hendean was putting new ads in the papers and getting flyers and posters printed. "Maybe you can talk to him tomorrow, hey?"

"Sure," Richard said, and asked him to show them where the woman had crash-landed.

Guestin didn't seem too eager, but he led them outside to the launch lip and pointed to a spot three-quarters of the way down. "Clearing, see it? Right there. Mr. Hendean was standing right here, he told me. Saw her go down, radioed to Nora, got the ambulance moving right away." He scratched at his chin, looked to Richard, and added, "If you kind of hunker down, Mister, it's easier. Hey, don't want you to fall." The edge of the ridge was marked with boulders, trees, and high weeds. When Richard did as the man suggested, he realized he'd been right—it was easier for some reason, and he was able to look down the mountain's thickly wooded side without suffering the vertigo that had slipped over him before.

The vertical drop ended when the side flared out like a skirt, but he reckoned it was still a good fifteen hundred feet before that happened. Through the trees he could see the tiny clearing Guestin had pointed out, the road that followed the mountain's base, and what looked like a doll's house just beyond, with a dark-red shed on a yard that looked to be three or four acres. Nora was Nora Costo, Hendean's ground manager. The gliders landed in either that yard, or the mowed field to its right, she gathered them up, put them in a van, and had them brought back to the summit if they were going to make another trip.

She was also a paramedic.

She was the one who had first seen the body.

Richard looked north and south along the slope as far at the forest would permit, and wondered if Trish McCormick would have lived if she had landed where she should have instead of where she did.

"What was he doing, just waiting around for someone to land?" Joanne wanted to know.

He doubted it. Like the guard in the park, the woman had most likely been in the wrong place at the wrong time. The more he looked, the more he understood that the area was a perfect place for the rogue—enough people and animals around to hunt, enough wilderness to hide in.

He knows it well, Richard decided. No wonder he's been able to stay free for so long.

He knows this place like the back of his hand.

The wind nudged him from behind then, spilling hair into his eyes. He swiped at it absently, backed away, and rose. He thanked Guestin for his help, and smiled to himself as the man nodded politely but gave most of his attention to Joanne, and most of that to her chest. He would have said something when she joined him in the car, but he had a feeling she would probably belt him a good one.

"Now what?" she asked, leaving Leon's Air behind. "Do you want to see that clearing?"

He shook his head. "Won't do any good." At least, not in daylight, he thought. He rubbed his forehead, blew out a breath, and checked his watch.

It was going on four.

The sun was already on its way down, and the cloud cover had given the mountain an early twilight.

"You want to drop in on the Costo woman?" She tapped an impatient finger on the steering wheel. "Maybe you can find out something she saw that she doesn't know she saw." She chuckled. "If you see what I mean."

"Later," he answered, keeping his tone neutral. "First thing is, I have to check in with Washington. Could we go back to the hotel?"

"I'll drop you off."

"Do you have to? After all this, I was kind of hoping I could treat you to a drink, or dinner."

She looked at him sourly, and he grimaced. "I do have a job, you know," she reminded him. "The desk shit, remember?"

He nodded.

"Tell you what, though," she said as they reached town, "We'll stay away from that other road. We'll go down the back way."

"Okay. Whatever you say."

"Yeah, right."

There was more traffic now, and people on the sidewalks in hats and heavy coats. A black pickup waited at an intersection, and he stared at it, turned and looked through the rear window until it headed off in the opposite direction.

"This back way. Is it like the way up?"

"Worse," she said gleefully.

She was right.

*   *   *

The hotel was awash with people and noise when he stepped inside, so much so that Richard instantly forgot the harrowing downhill drive, and Joanne's smug expression when she let him out at the curb.

The lobby was packed, both with registration lines and movement, the noise level almost unbearably high. As he stood waiting for an elevator, he noticed that many had exchanged suits and jeans for what seemed to be costumes. He recognized a few *Star Trek* outfits, but little else. Capes and cloaks mixed with black leather and chains; Hollywood medieval with street corner grunge.

For no reason at all, it made him feel inexplicably old, and he was grateful when he was able to make it to the third floor. The relative silence was welcome, and he realized that if tonight was the rule rather than the exception, he would have to find another, quicker, way to get up and down. Two elevators for a thousand people wasn't satisfactory at all.

He slipped his key into the door, turned the handle, and froze.

A thousand people. Probably more.

Costumes that he imagined would grow more elaborate with time.

The rogue, he thought; my God, if it knew . . .

He entered the room cautiously, testing the air for the scent of invasion, relaxing only when he was positive there hadn't been another search. Then he dropped on the couch and stared blindly at the opposite wall, ignoring the chill of a tiny draft from the window at his back.

After a moment he slipped the tiny cloth bag from his pocket and opened it, spreading it over his thigh. Inside were three miniatures carved from stone, none more than half an inch high—an owl, a hawk, and, in gleaming black, Anubis.

His fingers brushed over them lightly.

His eyes closed.

His breathing grew shallow.

Within minutes the hotel had been swallowed by a black fog, and a black wind howled, and a voice wept with pain.

When his eyes opened again—green fire—he saw the familiar desert.

This time, however, he wasn't alone.

15

The far end of the restaurant, beyond the L-shaped bar and the grill, was two steps higher and slightly more narrow than the rest of the room, separated from it by a gleaming silver railing more symbolic than practical. It was large enough only for three round tables, two of which were empty.

Miles Blanchard sat at the third, in the window-side corner, watching the dinner patrons fill the booths, leave, fill them again, and patiently stand two deep at the bar. Some were obviously office workers, the rest those who had come to the convention. Eyeing each other while trying too hard not to look as if they were.

None approached him.

He was not in a good mood, and it must have shown no matter how hard he tried to keep his expression neutral.

Not an hour ago, he had seen Turpin enter the hotel, thoughtful and, perhaps, just a little shaken. Blanchard had walked right past him, could have touched him, could have killed him right then, had he wanted to; instead, he had come directly here, ordered what turned out to be a passable meal, and tried to figure out exactly what was going on.

Crimmins had been furious that the Strider hadn't been taken care of already. After a minute's pompous posturing, threats were made. Explanations were demanded. His voice had risen nearly to a woman's pitch. But each time Blanchard tried to speak, the old man cut him off.

There was something wrong here.

And when Blanchard, his own temper straining at the leash, reminded his employer that there was still a rogue on the loose as part of this ridiculous equation, Crimmins had exploded, ranting about forces Blanchard knew nothing of, forces not to be trifled with, not to be tempted, and certainly not to be questioned by "the likes of you, you ignorant little man."

The leash had slipped.

Blanchard hung up on him, and was out of the room before the telephone could ring again.

He was not really afraid of Crimmins, or that mysterious group the old fart represented; without being immodest, he knew he was too valuable for them to lose. It wasn't that he knew too much; he was simply too good. He doubted very seriously that they could find him should they underestimate his value, and should he decide it would be prudent to disappear.

Yet he hated to admit it, but Crimmins' tantrum had unnerved him somewhat, and it wasn't until he had finished the meal and his second drink that he was able to think straight. Or as straight as he could, considering how furious he still was.

A waitress glanced in his direction, and he lifted his empty tumbler. She smiled, nodded, and headed for the bar.

Not a good idea, he chided himself; three drinks,

and it's not even six. At this rate, he'd be flat on his ass before the night really began.

He snorted, grinned to himself, and inhaled slowly, deeply, stretching his arms above his head and lacing his fingers. He pushed, and his knuckles cracked, loudly. Then his shoulders. A doctor had once told him that was a great way to invite arthritis; Blanchard had taken offense and had cut the man badly. Used a scalpel, and sliced him across his knuckles. All of them.

The drink was delivered, and he cupped his hands around the tumbler, looking out over the heads of the diners and the drinkers, not really seeing them, not really listening.

What he hoped for was a revelation based on what little he already knew; what he expected was a visit from Wanda Strand, to let him know when Turpin was safely ensconced in his room.

He scowled.

There was another catch—Wanda.

Evidently Crimmins hadn't trusted him. She had been waiting when he had checked in, not saying much, just enough beyond a friendly greeting to let him know that with this assignment neither of them were going to fly solo.

He knew her.

Twice—once in London, once in San Diego—they had worked together. Not really partners, and certainly not close. But he had been forced to admit that they somehow actually managed to complement each other. If he was the Man of a Thousand Faces, she was unnervingly close to being a true Seer. She knew things, and after their first meeting, he never asked her how.

He didn't need to be a Seer to see the blood on her hands.

At the end of their lobby meeting that afternoon, she had leaned over and said, "Miles, they want us dead, you know. When this is done."

He hadn't responded right away, because he hadn't believed it then, and he didn't really believe it now. They may want him dead, but it wasn't going to happen. As he'd decided only a few minutes ago, he was too good, and they needed him too badly.

Wanda was apparently a different story.

It was also apparent she wasn't all that concerned.

Which is why he also figured he would live longer than she.

Pride, as he remembered his Bible, goeth not before a fall, as was so often misquoted; it goeth before destruction.

His lips twitched.

He looked down at his drink and studied the color of it, the red of it.

Five minutes later he took the first sip, having already decided that it was time, tonight, for the bloodbath to begin.

He glanced to his right, to a narrow glass door that led directly into the lobby. It was so innocuous, hardly anyone used it. A good way to watch the passing crowds. A good way to keep track of who entered and left the elevators.

A better way to mark the first victim.

The sun held no heat, and there were no shadows on the sand.

Despite the strong wind that forced him to squint, not a grain shifted.

He wandered among the ruins until he located the source of the weeping, and stood on the crumbling threshold of a doorway wide enough to let an army pass. Ahead was an interior garden, all the flowers and bushes gone save for a single stone vase on a dark stone table. In the vase was a red rose, and its thorns were gleaming crimson.

The woman sat at the table, watching him, eyes puffed and reddened, hands clasped and trembling, wearing a single thin garment the wind rippled like white water.

"Fay?" He took a step toward her.

Fay Parnell shook her head violently.

Her tears were black, and streaked her cheeks blackly.

"Fay."

There was movement behind him.

Wanda left the elevator on the gallery floor. She had exchanged her topcoat for a lightweight cardigan with pockets deep enough to hold her cigarettes and lighter; on her feet were what appeared to be black ballet slippers. After a moment's indecision, she moved ahead to the latticework railing and looked down into the lobby.

Miles wasn't there.

Facing the elevators again, she glanced left and right, ignoring the scores of people wandering past her, most not looking, one or two young men trying to catch her eye. It almost made her smile.

A silent sigh, then, and she made for the four low steps to the elevators' left, part of them covered by a portable wheelchair ramp. She stepped up and walked down the middle of the wide hall, slowly, not caring when people had to squeeze past her, muttering and glaring. To her left was a marble staircase that led down to the first floor and, she knew, the restaurant entrance.

It wasn't what she wanted.

A few yards father on another, shorter wide corridor

opened to the left, at the end of which was a huge room. By the tables and chairs she could see, and longer tables at the back piled with provisions, she gathered this was some sort of refreshment area.

It still wasn't what she wanted.

Another ten yards, however, and she stopped.

The corridor ended in a T, with hotel offices directly ahead, and on the left, in the corner, the fire door which, if its current use was any indication, was a favorite mode of travel for those too impatient to wait for the elevators.

She stepped through the door, onto a gray painted concrete landing, heard hollow voices in the stairwell above and below, and made her way up one flight, to the third floor and through the doorway there.

This hall was long, and muted voices came from open doors far down to the right. The hall ended on her left, and she ducked around the corner and leaned back against the wall, staring at the door directly opposite her.

He was there.

In there.

The question was, how pissed would Miles be if she ended it all here and now?

Very, she decided, and grunted a quiet laugh.

Her right hand slipped into the pocket of her slacks, fingers curling around a short wand of engraved ivory inlaid with silver stars.

A knock, mock confusion—"I'm so sorry, I've got the wrong room, please forgive me."—and it would be over before Turpin knew what had hit him.

Just as she straightened, however, the double doors of the suite immediately to the left swept open, and a dozen people swarmed out, laughing, chattering, passing her with broad smiles and nods. One of them, a man about her height with thick white hair, paused, looked at her chest and said, "You'd better get your ID badge, Miss, or these security folks will hassle you all night."

She didn't know what to say and so nodded a mute thank-you, and damned whoever he and his friends were because Turpin couldn't possibly have missed all that commotion. She had never met the Strider, but she knew his reputation; whether he felt threatened or not, all his senses would be alerted.

Damn it, she thought; goddamn it.

Marcus Spiro glanced at the attractive woman leaning against the wall, thought to speak to her again, but was grabbed by the elbows and propelled around the corner and down the main hall. When he protested with a laugh, he was reminded, that the convention leaders wanted to speak to him before the opening ceremonies. Which meant now. And since they had paid his way, he couldn't very well ignore them.

Still, that woman—

Well, at least his keeper wasn't around.

Not fair, he chided himself. Leon wasn't a keeper. Every major guest was assigned someone whose job it was to keep the guest happy, and make sure he got to all the functions on time. The best ones, and Leon had turned out to be one of them, stayed the hell out of the way, like an unobtrusive waiter, just waiting for a look to bring him running.

Not a bad life for a weekend.

Thinking of his declining sales, Marcus sighed, wishing life could be that way all the time again.

As it was, coming down here every couple of years—

A young woman dropped out of the crowd ahead and grabbed his left arm. She wore a vivid red tank top, and jeans he figured must have taken her an hour to get into. When she tugged on his arm, he leaned down, listened for a moment, and straightened suddenly with a mock, "That's disgusting!", and an equally mock look of indignation.

"Sure is," she said, grinning. "So?"

He grinned and let her guide him toward the convention's operations center. Say what you will about traveling to towns like this in the middle of winter, having to put up with barely bathed cretins who slobbered all over you just so you'll autograph one of your books . . . say what you will about barely edible convention food, obscenely late nights, equally obscene early mornings, and the strain it put on a body whose sole exercise consisted of depositing royalty checks twice a year . . . say what you will about all of it, these things were still a great place to get yourself laid.

A glance over his shoulder was just in time to catch that other woman slipping through the fire door.

A glance down at the buxom woman beside him, giggling as she leaned into him, just to be sure he knew that what she had wasn't padded.

Oh well, he thought; a bird in the hand is almost as good as a bird in the bed.

He laughed aloud.

The others laughed with him.

The desert wind died.

He turned to see who it was who had followed him, but there was no one there. Nothing moved.

When he turned back, he nearly cried out—Fay was gone, the chair empty.

He hurried toward the table, calling her name, listening to the flat echo of his calls ricochet off the crumbling walls. There were no footprints in the sand, no sign she had even been here except, when he looked closely, for the splatter of a single black tear on the table.

He shivered, rubbed his arms for warmth, and called her name again.

No one answered.

Not even the wind.

But he wasn't alone, and that wasn't right.

This was his place, and his place only. When he needed the calm of meditation, when he needed answers for the hunt, when he needed reassurance that being a Silent Strider was neither a curse nor a condemnation, this is where he came.

And he always came alone.

Now, as he slumped dejectedly into the chair, he had one answer, and it tore at his heart as surely as a blade of silver:

Fay was dead.

How or why, he didn't know, but she was dead. His best friend was gone, a former lover, and there was no one to replace her.

He touched a finger to the tear, but it was dry. Dust. And when the wind returned, the tear scattered and was gone.

The rose remained, crimson thorns, scarlet petals.

He sat, and he stared at it until a shadow blocked the sun.

He looked up, unsmiling.

"You took her," he accused bitterly. "She had plenty of time yet, and you took."

"No," said Anubis. "She was brought to me."

Blanchard half rose when he saw Wanda weave through the crowd at the restaurant's entrance, raised a glass until she spotted him, and sat again, spreading his arms in greeting when she took the chair opposite him.

"Something to eat?"

"It was your invitation," she said blandly.

"What do you want?"

"Whatever. As long as it comes with wine. Lots of it."

He didn't ask what bothered her; he assumed it was the constant flow of people, constantly talking and laughing, here and there tucked into corners for intense conversation; holding books and posters and cups of beer and soda; staring at him, reading his name tag and frowning as they tried to place the name with the face they had never seen before.

He pointed to her chest. "You haven't registered."

"You're the second person to tell me that tonight." She took a cigarette from her pocket, lit it, and blew a stream of smoke at the ceiling. "I am not going to waste my money."

"Your funeral," he said, beckoning the waitress with a finger and a smile.

"Not quite," she answered.

He raised an eyebrow, but again didn't respond. He did, however, smell trouble, and he cursed Crimmins for sticking him with this woman. Nevertheless, he kept his expression as pleasant as he could, saying little while she ate, drinking two glasses of wine before her plate was clear.

Then she twisted around to look through the window at the deserted street, slumped back, and said, "God, it feels like midnight already." She squinted at a thin gold watch on her wrist. "Jesus H., it's barely seven."

"You're too edgy," he scolded lightly. The implication went deeper: you're supposed to be a pro, bitch, get it together before you get one of us killed. Not, he added silently; that I give a damn about you.

She looked at him for a long time with one eye half closed. Nodded slowly. Lit another cigarette. Stared at the glowing tip. "He's in his room now."

Blanchard waited.

"What don't we just do it and get it over with?"

It was a question, but just barely.

He wondered if she honestly knew who they were up against; he decided immediately he didn't give a damn because, no matter how it ended, she wasn't going to survive anyway. She got on his nerves. He hated people who got on his nerves.

"What are you going to do, bust in the door?" he said, not bothering to mask the sarcasm.

"Key."

His eyes widened slightly. "You have a key?"

"Nope."

"Then—"

Her smile was chilling. "Sugar, just follow me. There isn't a man's room in the world I can't get into. One way or the other."

16

Richard sat at the table, in the ruins, in the desert, and wept without tears.

. . . she was brought to me.

No translation needed: Fay Parnell had been murdered.

There was no one left on his side, now.

No one.

Not even the Warders.

It didn't take a genius, or the import of his dreams, to figure out that they knew full-well he wouldn't survive this assignment. Rogues, when all was said and done, could not be captured. Could not be taken prisoner. Could only be neutralized in one, lethal, way.

They had known it, and they had known how it would be long before he realized it himself.

He reached for the rose, but didn't touch it.

So what did they expect him to do, give his life to protect the Veil? To preserve their secrets? Were they counting on his tribe's dedication to the Garou to commit virtual suicide for them?

If he couldn't figure that out, he surely would die.
And dying, now, was the last thing on his mind.

It's a pisser, thought Curly Guestin; a real pisser,
staying here to all hours, busting my butt and no
overtime, no thanks, no bonus, no nothing.

He stomped around the large room, cleaning up,
wiping his tools and putting them away, making sure
the cabinets and chests were properly locked, making sure the silent alarms were ready to go as soon
as he left.

Shivering when the wind came through the zillion
cracks in the goddamn walls and ceiling.

It was like working in a barn.

Above him, the wings fluttered and rustled,
sounding like bats disturbed in their caves.

The frames swayed and twisted slowly, their faint
shadows on the whitewashed walls expanding and
shrinking as if they were running up to him and sliding away. Teasing. Taunting. He had seen it a million
times, but tonight, like last night, the night before,
and every night for the past week, he couldn't help
thinking that he didn't like them very much anymore.
They were spooky. They had never been spooky
before, but they were damn spooky now.

Ever since that blonde lady had been killed, those
shadows had been spooky.

It wasn't too bad when Leon was around, or one
of his buddies from down in the city. But too often,
ever since summer, Leon had started taking off early,
and Curly's buddies had been working double, triple
overtime just to make ends meet. He hardly saw
them at all anymore.

That left him alone when the sun went down.

Spooky; too damn spooky.

He slapped a rag over his table to knock the filings and bits of stiff thread onto the floor. He did it again, this time pretending he was knocking Leon silly, and the idea of him doing that to a man that size made him giggle so hard that he could barely stand up.

Not that he'd really want to hurt his boss. Leon was okay most of the time. When he wasn't brooding about something or other, when he wasn't complaining about his competition up the road, when he wasn't talking out loud about maybe closing the place down and moving down to Florida where he would lie on the beach all day and let women in little bathing suits bring him drinks until he died.

Curly didn't like that kind of talk.

It made him nervous, real nervous, because it had taken him a hell of a long time to find this job, and he didn't want to have to go through all that again, reading the papers, talking to people who thought he was so much older than he was because of his stupid hair. He didn't want to, and when he scolded his boss, Leon would look at him like he was from another planet.

"What the hell's the matter with you, man?" he would say. "Shit, if I do leave, you can have this goddamn place, okay? Knock yourself out, Curly, knock yourself out."

Curly slapped the table a third time, and stuffed the rag into his hip pocket. Then he stomped over to the door and grabbed his broom.

He didn't have to do it; playing janitor wasn't part of what he had been hired for. He was supposed to keep the frames and air foils working, that was all, keep the dopes who wanted to jump off the mountain from killing themselves on the way down.

He was a mechanic, an artist, and a genius with his tools. Being a janitor had never been his dream.

He did it anyway, though, because Leon sure as hell wouldn't. Curly hated coming in every morning and seeing crap all over. It didn't feel right. He had told Leon that a hundred million times every day practically when it wasn't done—it didn't feel right. Didn't look right, either, when the customers came in, saw the place looking like a junkyard after a tornado.

Leon didn't care.

All he cared about was watching people fly.

That's all he did. All day. Stood on the edge, hands in his pockets, and watched the people fly. Saying nothing. Humming to himself. Once in a while raking a couple of fingers through that goofy beard of his. Watching. Humming.

And collecting the money.

Curly looked around the room just to be sure everything was in its place, then switched on the tinny plastic radio he kept on the bench near the door. It only got one station. Tonight it was Suzy Bogguss singing about how wives don't like old girlfriends, and girlfriends don't like old wives.

"True enough," he said to the shadows as he attacked the floor. "Fucking true enough."

Right about now, he needed a new girlfriend himself, because his wife sure wasn't putting out these days. She was a sweet lady, and he supposed he probably kind of loved her a little, but long about last Thanksgiving she'd gone with her aunt up to Nashville, gotten herself religion again, and fornication had suddenly become out of the question.

"Jesus," he'd once exploded in frustration, "you ain't a nun, you know, Annie. Jesus, gimmie a break."

She hadn't liked that at all. In fact, for his blasphemy, she had made him sleep on the back porch for half a damn week. Him and the damn dogs.

He sighed, swept, listened to the wind pound the walls and wolf-howl in the eaves.

Now that police lady today, she was pretty okay for a police lady. Dark-red hair, a figure he couldn't keep his eyes off. He wondered if she had handcuffs. He wondered if she used them.

He giggled.

He swept.

That FBI guy, though, he was something else. Weird eyes. Kind of quiet. Moved like he was on tiptoe or something. Not a really big man, but he had a voice that sounded like it started somewhere at the bottom of a well. Not deep so much as full.

Really weird eyes.

He paused for a moment, sneezed, wiped his face with the back of a hand, thought about the police lady, and rolled his eyes as he got back to work.

Singing loudly and out of tune while Patsy sang about falling to pieces and not having the sense God gave her to do something about it.

Something slammed into the wall, and the lights began to flicker.

Joanne stood on the steps of police headquarters and zipped up her denim jacket. With chin tucked, she squinted at the sky, hoping to see at least one star, but the city lights cast a glow that showed her nothing but clouds.

A righteous shoot; that's what Lt. Millson had told her not half an hour ago. No charges, no penalties; Internal Affairs had closed the file, and she had been completely vindicated without prejudice, no blight on her record. Righteous shoot. She grunted. The man was from Chicago; they talked funny that way. Still, being exonerated ought to have been more . . . fulfilling, more satisfying somehow.

It only made her angry that the process had to have been gone through at all.

She stepped slowly down to the pavement, momentarily confused about where she had parked her car. Which reminded her of Richard Turpin, and that made her scowl. Her desk duty had been lifted, but she was still assigned to the mystery guy from D.C.; when she had demanded an explanation, all she'd gotten was a look.

"He doesn't tell me anything," she had complained. "We did some looking today, talked to the girl and some guy at the hang-gliding place, and he doesn't tell me anything."

"He doesn't have to," Millson said, not unsympathetically.

"Well, how the hell am I supposed to help him, then?"

"Don't shoot him."

Her smile was screw-you-sour, her departure swift, and she still couldn't figure out exactly what the hell she was supposed to do. Be a damn chauffeur? Get him in bed, find out all he knows? Beat the shit out of him, find out all he knows? Jesus. Ten years a cop and this is what she gets?

And why the hell hadn't she told the lieutenant about the truck?

In the beginning, she had been excited, even eager, when she had been assigned to the task force hunting for the Lookout Mountain killer. Most of the work was dull, to be sure—door to door, asking questions, correlating interviews, asking more questions—but then there were the results, the hints, the ghosts of answers maddeningly close and maddeningly out of reach, staring at charts and paper until her eyes burned as she and a dozen others willed a pattern to make itself known.

A pattern was knowledge.

With knowledge came possible prediction of the next killing.

She had been to all the sites, and wondered why Turpin hadn't taken the time today to visit the one on the side of the mountain. Instead, he had spent most of his time talking to Polly Logan, and it wasn't until she had returned to headquarters that she realized he hadn't told her what he had learned.

And he had definitely learned something.

She had seen it in his eyes.

She had half a mind to return to the Read House, corner that spook or whatever the hell he really was, and choke him until he stopped playing games and told her.

It wasn't fair; she was a good cop, and getting better, and it damn well wasn't fair.

She started in one direction, realized she was wrong, made an about-face, and nearly bumped into two uniforms complaining about the mechanics in the motor pool, how they never get anything right, and the uniforms get all the grief when something falls off a car.

She walked on, muttering to herself, working herself into a mood that soon enough had her deciding that, half a mind or not, she would see Turpin tonight and demand some answers to some questions.

He rose and walked away, leaving the table and the rose behind. In the far corner of the garden was a crumbling stone staircase, debris scattered at its base, unmoved by the wind. He climbed to the top and looked over the wall, and all the ruined, blasted walls that surrounded him.

Now the wind did reach him, tugging his hair back and away, pressing his shirt and trousers to his skin. Howling. Forever howling.

And the sun in the green-streaked sky felt like a match held against his flesh.

But inside, where it counted, he was cold.

Curly gaped at the lights, stared at the wall where he thought he heard the noise. The wind was busting the outside something fierce, it could be a branch or something that got flung against the shed.

Or, he thought miserably, it could be one of the metal trash cans got loose. If it had, he'd have to fetch it before the wind rolled it off the mountain. They hardly cost anything, but Leon always complained whenever they got dented.

Grumbling, shaking his head, he propped the broom against the workbench and went to the door.

It was cold out there, freezing; he could feel it through the wood.

Another thump, not as loud as the first, and he realized his hands were shaking a little.

"Oh, Lord, Curly, you scared of a little noise?"

He forced a laugh and yanked the door open, stepped outside, and threw up a hand to protect his face when a flurry of dead leaves leapt out of the dark. He rolled his eyes, and moaned when he saw the trash can shuddering down the length of the building, nudged by the wind. It didn't take but a few seconds to catch it, and a few seconds more to drag it back inside. He'd fix it in its place tomorrow; tonight he wanted to get the hell out, get home, get showered, kiss his wife, and get the hell to the bar to meet his girl and get laid.

By the time he had grabbed up his broom again,

the lights had steadied, and Emmylou on the radio was whining about Amarillo and something about a jukebox.

He didn't much care for the song, but he sang along anyway, making up the words he didn't know, making up the notes he couldn't quite reach.

Not that it mattered.

As long as the duet kept him from listening to the quiet, measured thumping along the wall by the door.

Blanchard was impressed.

They had made their way easily through the lobby throng, smiling and nodding as if they were royalty, as if they belonged. Once they reached the front desk, far to the left away from a handful still checking in, Wanda had leaned her elbows on the polished wood counter, looked at a young man flipping through some cards, and her voice deepened, became smooth and thick as Georgia syrup.

"Excuse me," she said, craned her neck so she could read the clerk's gold nameplate on his blue-blazer chest. "Lane, sugar, could you help me a second?"

"Jesus," Blanchard muttered, then yelped when she kicked back with a heel and caught him on the shin. The pain was sharp and deep, and as he gasped for a breath, she turned with a smile, following his gaze down to the innocuous black ballet slippers. "Tempered steel around the rim," she told him, still smiling. "Specially made."

He swallowed, but couldn't quite manage a smile. "I'd love to have him make something for me."

"Too late. Poor man died suddenly at a very young age." Then she turned her attention back to the clerk. "My key," she said, the syrup flowing smoothly. "My husband, he goes out on the town, says, 'Darlin', meet me here, be dressed to kill.'" She straightened and spread her arms slightly, her expression now rueful. "Not exactly ready to kill, am I."

"You look fine to me, ma'am," the clerk answered, just shy of flirtation.

"Well, you know how it is, we women and all." She looked troubled. "Problem is, the man took the key, and how am I going to get into the shower, get myself ready before he comes back?"

"No problem, ma'am. I can make another one up for you in a second. And you're Mrs. . . ?"

"Turpin," she answered without missing a beat. "Richie Turpin."

Blanchard turned away quickly before he choked, only half listening as she kept up the chatter to keep the clerk from checking the records too closely. Amazing, he thought. It was as if he had left the restaurant with one woman, and had ended up here with someone else, someone infinitely more seductive.

He was truly impressed.

More so when she thanked the clerk with a smile that damn near made him blush, whirled and walked by, holding the key up and grinning. "You ready?"

He touched his jacket at the breast. "Always."

"Wonderful." She linked her arm with his. "In and out, and then we go." An overweight woman in a costume more skin than cloth bumped into her and apologized with a laugh. Without a glance in her direction, Wanda shoved her away. "Christ, I hate this fucking city."

Curly swept the pile of dust and crap his broom had gathered over to the door. Ordinarily he would have used the little broom and the dust pan now to pick it up, and drop it in the metal trash barrel outside. Not tonight. Leon had left him alone all damn day, nobody to talk to but the birds, the wings in the rafters, and those cops. Fuck the dust, he wanted to go home.

If he had any brains, he'd quit come morning, let Leon do his own damn work.

If he had any brains, which Leon kept telling him he didn't. All the time.

He grabbed the broom in a strangle-hold, kicked open the door, and barely had time to catch his breath before the wind slammed into him, scattering the dust back across the floor.

His shoulders slumped. "Aw . . . shit." He let the broom fall. "Come on, Curly, you stupid or something? Use your head, huh? Jesus."

He stared at the mess helplessly, wiped a hand over his face, and kicked at the floor.

The hell with it; he'd do it in the morning.

He grabbed the edge of the door to slam it closed, and barely registered the thing that whipped out of the black to slash across his chest.

"Jesus!" he yelled, and stumbled backward, looking dumbly at the coveralls hanging in shreds down to his belly. "Jesus God!"

He didn't feel the pain until the dark came inside and ripped out his throat.

By then it was too late.

He was sprawled on his back, on the floor, praying as hard as he had ever prayed in his life.

Not to be spared.

Just to die.

The pain was awful, almost too much to feel, but it wasn't as bad as the teeth that tore open his stomach, as the red eyes that watched him, and he could swear they were smiling.

Please, Lord, he thought; please, Lord, please.

But it didn't happen.

17

Marcus Spiro was in the ballroom, at the top of the gallery. He was seated at a long, white cloth-covered table on a raised platform with the rest of the convention's guests, most of whom seemed to wish they were somewhere else.

He smiled.

He had arrived late, panting a little, and twice he had counted the number of people in the theater-style setup, and couldn't get more than fifty, no matter how hard he tried. Fifty out of what? A thousand, at least? Fifteen hundred? Not that he was surprised. Every convention he had ever been to was like this—they had opening ceremonies, nobody came, the few who did applauded politely, then everyone headed for the nearest room party.

It was a joke.

He smiled at them all as if they were his closest, long-lost friends.

He looked toward the back and saw Leon standing behind the last row, still wearing an anorak, cheeks faintly red. Late, too, but that was all right, because that big oaf understood that a man had to be alone once in a while, and he asked no embarrassing questions whose answers would have to be lies. He hated lying. It caused too many complications.

A faint noise made him shift his gaze down to the first row, at the woman in her tank top, she called herself Pear, who saw his discomfort and leaned forward a little. A reminder.

He smiled at her, praying that the evening wouldn't be wasted.

Christ, he thought, I hate this fucking stuff.

Joanne had been at the Read House a number of times, officially and not, and she could see at a glance that using the elevator to get to the third floor would be a waste of time. She was too impatient for that. Instead, she took the fire stairs at a run, slammed through the fire door, and rounded the corner.

She stood in front of 303 and pressed a hand to her chest while she caught her breath.

Be there, she willed, and knocked as she raked a hand through her wind-rumpled hair.

He didn't answer.

The halls were quiet.

She knocked again, harder, and this time called his name.

He didn't answer.

Okay, maybe this was a mistake. Maybe she had no right to barge in on him like this. Maybe she ought to be a good little girl and play by the rules. He wasn't here to help in the investigation; he was here to run an investigation on his own. No problem. She was a cop, he wasn't, and who the hell are you kidding, girl?

She slammed a fist against the door, glaring at the peephole, daring him to look out and ignore her.

He didn't answer.

Damn it, where the hell are you?

To her left and around the corner, she heard the metallic creak of the fire door opening, quiet voices sounding hollow in the stairwell beyond.

Then Turpin's door opened slowly, and she didn't wait for an invitation. She pushed her way in without bothering with an apology, frowned briefly at the darkened room, and strode to the couch, standing between it and the coffee table, facing the street, arms folded across her chest.

"We have to talk, Turpin," she said tightly, not turning around.

"Yes. Yes, we do."

Blanchard closed his eyes, searching for calm. His lips moved in a litany of obscenities, but he didn't make a sound.

Wanda didn't bother to keep silent, and she didn't bother to temper her language. In her left hand was the ivory wand, which she tapped angrily against her leg.

"We should go in anyway," she said at last.

He shook his head emphatically.

"Why not? Two of us, two of them. Jesus Christ, Miles or whatever the hell you're calling yourself these days, what's the goddamn problem?"

His eyes snapped open.

She backed away, but not fast enough. He grabbed her upper arm and squeezed it, hard, as he yanked her away from the corner. Heat swept over his face. He pulled her so close she had to lean her head back to focus on his eyes.

"She," he said tightly, "is a cop, remember? A detective. We take care of him, there's no real problem. We include the bitch, we'll have the whole fucking force crawling all over the damn place."

Her gaze was steady, no emotion at all. "What's your point? We'll be long gone by the time they find them."

He tried to speak, couldn't, tried again and failed, and finally flung her away, so hard her head bounced off the wall and her knees almost buckled at the impact.

But she didn't blink. Not once.

"Messy," was all he could bring himself to say. "I don't like messy. Messy makes for messy questions. Messy questions sometimes get real answers." Then, for good measure, he added, "Crimmins."

The ivory slipped back into her pocket. She adjusted her cardigan, ran a smoothing palm down her blouse, and brushed by him, heading toward the elevator alcove.

"I'm going to the bar," she said. "Call me when you find out where you left your balls."

A tree had been planted at the curb outside the window, its branches merging with the early night. There were no cars that she could see, nothing but streetlights and reflections and the Chubb Building in the distance, glowing red, like sullen fire.

All her anger and impatience had instantly drained at the sound of his voice, but she couldn't turn around.

The room was still dark; she didn't want to see his face in what dim light there was.

Footfalls behind her; he was pacing, not wearing shoes.

"I'm sorry," he said quietly. "I . . . I've had some bad news."

She nodded.

"My, uh, best friend . . . her name is Fay . . ." A soft exhalation; he cleared his throat harshly. "Was Fay. She's dead."

"I'm sorry. An accident?"

"Murder."

She did look over her shoulder then. He had dropped into a chair at the table, legs spread, one arm on the table, the other in his lap. The outside light didn't reach far enough—it looked as if he had no head. There was a glint, however, to mark his eyes. They looked almost green.

"Murder," he repeated dully.

She recognized then what she had heard in his voice—he'd been crying, or fighting so hard not to that the result was the same—he was hoarse, barely sounded human.

Bracing one hand against the sofa's back, she lowered herself onto the cushion, pushing into the corner, one leg up, one foot on the floor. She winced when her beeper dug into her thigh, unclipped it from her belt and placed it on the end table without looking. "Not . . . not your wife?"

A sad laugh. "No. No, we weren't . . . we couldn't."

Helplessness prevented her from asking more questions simply because she didn't know the right questions to ask.

He leaned forward into the light, forearms on his knees, staring at the floor. "Look, Jo, it's . . ." Another laugh, this one bitter while he shook his head. "It's been less than two days, and I've done nothing but treat you like you aren't even here. You probably won't believe it, but that's really not my style."

She tilted her head in a half shrug. "You've been a shit, more or less."

"More or less."

"And you know a lot more than we do. About this killer, I mean."

"Oh, yes." He looked up without raising his head. "Oh, yes."

She settled deeper in the corner and pulled her other leg up, hooked fingers around the ankle to keep it in place. "Do you know who he is?"

"I don't even know yet if he's a he."

She shook her head doubtfully. "No offense, but a woman generally doesn't commit crimes like this. Like they say, it's not really in the profile."

He looked at the floor again before scratching fiercely through his hair. "For the time being, you'll have to take my word for it—there is no profile for the kind of madman we're after."

Her mouth opened, closed quickly, and she gripped her ankle more tightly. The room felt unusually warm, but a chill slithered across her shoulders anyway, making her shift them until it dissipated. When he sat up slowly, his face retreating into shadow, she could almost hear the pain, almost felt it with him. That bothered her. She didn't know this man at all, had no idea who he was or where he was from, so there was no reason at all why he should affect her this way.

No reason at all.

But he did.

The silence expanded, but it wasn't uncomfortable. What questions she had—and there were dozens—would have to wait. In his own good time, she knew; in his own good time.

In the main hall outside, a voice called and another answered.

A truck backfired to a halt at the traffic light below the window, gears grinding, brakes hissing.

His chair creaked as he shifted.

The room no longer felt too warm, but a peculiar scent remained, dry heat and hot sand. She blinked slowly, almost sleepily.

"You're very good," he said suddenly, quietly.

She started, and bit back a yelp.

"At waiting, I mean."

"I have to be." And she did. Often, interrogation yielded more just by sitting there, not looking at but watching the person who had the answers she was after. By saying little, or nothing at all, she could elicit outrage, then denial, outrage again, and finally, if she was lucky, a slow crumbling of defenses that often told her more than words.

"So do I." He left his chair, took his time moving to the opposite corner of the couch, angling his body so he could see her without having to turn his head. Because of the furniture's size, there wasn't much more than a foot between them.

More calling in the hall, and an outburst of explosive laughter that lasted for several seconds.

"Listen, Jo—"

"How did you know?" she demanded sharply.

"What?"

"Jo. How did you know to call me Jo? Hardly anyone does anymore. You did it before, too."

A one-shoulder shrug. "I don't know. It feels right." A momentary frown. "Sorry if it offends you."

She waved him off—*it doesn't*—and squirmed a little to regroup.

This was crazy. She wanted to reach out, touch his leg, so much so that she clasped her hands in her lap and forced them to stay there.

"I have a problem, Joanne," he said.

"Jo."

He smiled. "Okay. I have a problem, Jo, and it goes beyond what your superiors might have told you." He gazed out the window, staring and seeing nothing, one arm resting along the back of the couch.

"If it'll make you feel any better, they've told me squat."

He chuckled. "That's because they don't know squat. About me, that is. What I do."

"So? What do you do?"

A finger lifted. "That is the problem." The finger pointed at the window. "Out there is a killer. He, maybe she, is insane and getting worse. He's going to kill again, I don't know when, and I'm supposed to stop him."

She shuddered, and pulled her lower lip thoughtfully between her teeth. When he said "stop," she had a bad feeling he didn't mean "catch."

"Son of a bitch," she whispered suddenly. Then, louder, "Son of a bitch." She straightened. "You're not official, are you?" It wasn't a question, it was an accusation.

He turned toward her, sliding the left side of his face into the room's shadow.

As if he were wearing a mask, she thought, and didn't like it.

"You're not government at all. FBI, CIA, something like that, I mean." She sat even straighter. "Goddammit, Turpin, you're a *civilian*." The heat of her indignation began to creep into her face. "What the hell is going on around here? Who the hell has that kind of pull?"

She started to rise, but he leaned over and placed a hand on her leg. Not hard. Enough to stop her.

"My problem," he said evenly. "It's no exaggeration, Jo, to say that if I tell you what you want to know, even just a little, things aren't ever going to be the same for you again. Ever. I guarantee it."

She wouldn't have believed him if it hadn't been

for the clear reluctance in his voice, and the sadness she could see in those strange eyes. As it was, the matter-of-fact way he spoke unnerved her more than what he had actually said.

She rubbed her throat lightly. "I gather we can't go on until you do tell me."

"I don't think so. Not and be very effective."

"And if you don't anyway?"

"You'll have to tell your lieutenant. You'll have to protest more than you probably already have."

She nodded; he was right.

"And he'll have to order you to stick with me, because he doesn't know, either. He thinks this is all government work." A fleeting sardonic smile. "Official government, that is, covert or not. If you still refuse, he'll have to reassign you, take you off the task force. More. You won't like that, Jo. It'll be scut work. Shit work. Rookie work not even the rookies get to do. You'll be driven from the force.

"Sooner or later, they'll drive you out."

She knew the drill, knew what her record would say when it was over: uncooperative, making waves, and probably labeled unstable.

She very nearly laughed; she didn't, but her voice was bitter. "I get it. You don't tell me what's up, and I get the royal shaft. You tell me, and I'm probably not going to like it, and maybe get the shaft anyway. Plus, I'll probably be in some danger. Right?"

"No." He shook his head solemnly. "Not some danger. A lot of danger." His fingers slid along her leg and away. "There's a fair chance you won't live through it."

Angrily, she dusted the leg where the hand had been. "If you're trying to scare me off, Turpin, it isn't going to work. I have no intention of ever giving up being what I am, what I worked for, and I sure don't intend for some mystery man to—"

The beeper sounded behind her, and she jumped so violently, she nearly fell into his lap. When she looked up, their faces were only inches apart.

Eyes, she thought; those eyes . . . until he touched her shoulder, reminding her of the summons. She whirled, then, and grabbed the receiver from the telephone on the table. After getting an outside line, she dialed the station's number, identified herself, listened, and hung up almost immediately.

"Let's go," she said, getting quickly to her feet.

He looked at her quizzically.

"There's been another one. And the body's still fresh."

18

. . . blood . . .

Joanne had already slapped a magnetized red bubble on the roof of her car by the time Richard threw himself into the front seat. He barely had time to pull his feet in and close the door before she bolted through the red-light intersection, one hand on the steering wheel, the other holding a mike to her lips, letting the others know she was on the road and on the way.

She said nothing about him.

He winced as she veered sharply around a pair of slower cars, and held his breath when she leaned on the horn and nearly clipped the rear bumper of a pickup that had hesitated in the middle of the next intersection.

"Don't you have a siren?"

She shrugged with one shoulder. "Busted."

"Wonderful."

The radio crackled static; half the traffic was garbled, but what he did hear told him roadblocks were being set up throughout the city and around the mountain.

"It was that guy," she said, swinging into the left lane to pass a lumbering city bus.

"What guy?"

"That Curly guy. At the hang-gliding place."

Shit, he thought, and grabbed for the dashboard when she played matador at another crossing, this time with a moving van that seemed in no hurry to get out of her way until she blasted the horn.

The office buildings were left behind; warehouses now, barely illuminated, their lights brittle and wan. The neon on the handful of restaurants and bars seemed even more seedy, despite their supposedly cheery glow.

What he thought was a snowflake hit the windshield and melted.

Dead ahead, at the Y-intersection near the supermarket, he saw patrol cars parked at angles in the middle of the road, their lights flashing. Joanne slowed only a little to give them time to part and let her pass, then accelerated again.

"We'll take the same way. It's not as steep."

He grunted, wanting to close his eyes so he wouldn't see the blur of dark trees, or the way the city fell away so quickly from the alarmingly low guard rail. If there were streetlamps, he didn't see them; there was only the gray pull of the headlamps on the tarmac.

Seconds later, they reached the boulder outcropping, and he tensed as she took the curve around it without hesitation.

The way ahead was clear.

"I know what you're thinking," she said, manhandling the car around the final bend.

"I doubt it."

"You're thinking I'm a damn good driver, making it all this way without hitting a damn thing."

"We're not there yet."

She laughed. "We will be. You gotta have faith."

At the top, another roadblock. She passed it carefully, taking the road left, and speeding up again. It didn't take long for the houses to be left behind.

"A couple of minutes," she told him.

He squeezed the tiny bundle in his pocket, and nodded, wishing the radio chatter was more clear, but he could only catch one or two words at a time; everyone seemed to be talking at once, and he wondered how the hell anyone could pass on information that way.

The road dipped and climbed.

The infrequent houses on the left were lit top and bottom, and he caught glimpses of people clustered in their yards, all facing the same way. Figures moved among the trees, slashing the air with flashlight beams. At least two pairs of police dogs straining at their leashes, testing the ground and air.

"Not wasting any time," she noted, sounding pleased and frustrated at the same time.

They flashed by the college, windows alight, silhouettes against the panes, staring out.

"They don't have to be afraid now," Joanne said tightly. "He's already made his kill for the night."

"Maybe."

She stared at him for too long, he had to point at the road to redirect her attention. "What the hell do you mean by that?"

He wiped his face with a palm. "I mean, the pattern's broken. Shattered." He watched a silver glow in the sky, beyond the road's next rise. "He's gone over the edge. There's no way, now, to predict his next move."

"Swell."

The ridge flattened after the rise, and he saw the congestion at the staging area. At least half a dozen cruisers parked on both sides of the road, an ambulance backed up to the shed's door, men walking purposefully from one place to another while others just stood around, stamping their feet against the cold, hands tucked under their armpits. Breath steamed in the light thrown by headlamps and electric torches. As she braked to a skidding halt just past the shed, he saw the flutter of yellow crime-scene ribbon.

They hurried toward the entrance.

"You got that FBI ID?" she asked.

"Yes."

"Put it on your jacket. It'll save a lot of questions."

He did, scolding himself for forgetting such a simple thing.

But he couldn't help it.

His nostrils flared, and he inhaled deeply.

. . . blood . . .

Four men were on their hands and knees on the gravel, peering at the stones, one man behind them with a handful of tiny yellow flags. A trail of them reached from the threshold to where he stood.

Richard followed her under the tape, kept one step behind as several voices greeted her. Someone stepped out of the office, a stump of a man in a heavy, dark-blue jacket, the collar up. He wore no hat, but there were bars on the collar's wings.

"Lieutenant Millson," she told him out of the corner of his mouth. "My boss. Task-force head."

"He's the one who gave you to me?"

She looked up at him and grinned without mirth.

"Turpin, nobody gives me to nobody. I was assigned. There's a hell of a difference."

Past the door, near the cliff edge, he heard the sound of a man vomiting. Two white-coated attendants lounged against the ambulance, smoking.

Lt. Millson intercepted them before they could go inside. Joanne introduced Richard, who watched the man's face—small eyes and small mouth, with a large blunt nose between. Pudgy cheeks. Black hair matted around his forehead and ears. A toupee, he realized; it's a goddamn toupee.

Richard shook the policeman's gloved hand and hunched his shoulders against the cold wind. "Bad?" He nodded at the building.

"You've never seen it that bad, boy."

Oh, yes I have, he thought, but didn't say it aloud.

The call had come in less than half an hour ago. Nora Costo, Hendean's assistant below, had come up to see if she couldn't convince him to close down for a while. She was, the lieutenant said, tired of hanging around all day, without practically anyone to watch out for.

"She's over there." He pointed to a sedan twenty yards away. A small woman sat sideways on the front seat, hands cupped around a Styrofoam cup of coffee. A patrolwoman crouched beside her, talking softly. "Walked in, saw the . . . scene, called it in right away from her car. Lookout Mountain cops were on the roadblocks almost instantly."

Not soon enough, Richard thought; damn it, not soon enough.

He looked at the doorway, took a breath, and started for it.

"Hey," the lieutenant said. "I thought I said—"

Richard stared at him, stared at the hand reaching for his arm, and stepped inside. Behind him,

Joanne muttered something that may have been a curse or an apology, and followed.

"Aw, shit," she said. "Aw, Jesus."

Curly Guestin lay spread-eagled on his worktable.

What was left of him, that is.

Richard stepped carefully around the shimmering pools of blood and stood at the dead man's feet, hands in his pockets, breathing through his mouth. There wasn't much left of Guestin from the waist up; it looked as if someone had taken a hacksaw to him, slashing indiscriminately until his left arm had nearly been severed, his torso gutted from navel to throat, his face little more than a red mask.

. . . blood . . .
   . . . fresh blood . . .

Richard turned slowly, ignoring the men who worked around the room, trying to find something in the wreckage besides blood. Mumbling to themselves. Once in a while, gagging.

"Find out what you can," he said to Joanne, and before she could ask, he left, brushed past Millson, and moved stiffly toward the road.

He heard the lieutenant mutter, "Pussy," but didn't stop.

No time; he had no time.

Suddenly the beat of rotor blades overwhelmed the noise of radios and whispers, and a helicopter rose above the ridge, two intense white beams stretched below it like legs. Cops grabbed for their hats as a minor dust storm swept over the scene, causing the yellow ribbons to snap like whips. Richard used the momentary confusion to run back toward Joanne's car, past it, and duck into the trees.

He heard shouts, and froze until he realized they weren't meant for him.

Then he began to run.

No time.

. . . *merging* . . .

No time.

Slipping from trunk to trunk, angling toward the edge, shaking the scent of fresh human blood from his nostrils, searching for the other scent and nearly howling when he found it.

The rogue had come here, and had gone over the edge.

He clung to a small pine and looked down, frowning, seeing nothing but knowing this was the way the other one had gone.

Not that long ago.

Headlights flashed along the road far below; he could barely make out the distant wail of a siren. Four patrol cars, one of them pausing, then speeding up again, heading north toward the river. Although he couldn't see the woodland down there, he spotted several winks of light. The search party had begun to build even in the valley. He didn't have much time.

From somewhere near the shed, Joanne called his name.

The helicopter was joined by a second, and they swung off, northward, one on either side of the ridge.

"Damn it, Turpin!"

He slipped between two large rocks and began to climb-slide downward, letting the trees be his brakes, letting them swing him on to the next one. Mountain climbing in reverse, with no safety net.

The scent was still fairly strong—sweat and blood and a touch of outright fear. He puzzled at that, but couldn't concentrate on much more than not falling; the angle of the mountainside was such that losing his balance would mean slamming his way all the way to the bottom, or near enough that it wouldn't make any difference when they found him.

"Hey!" A young man's voice in the stand he'd just left. "Hey, down here!"

He snorted angrily.

"Here!" A wide slant of white bounced off the treetops, settled, and aimed down. "Here!"

Richard didn't stop.

Branches whipped at the thick fur that covered him head to claw; twice something dug at the corner of his eye, and whipping his head away made him dizzy for a second; his left foot lost its purchase, and he fell hard against a half-buried rock, the wind forced from his lungs.

"Down there, damn it! I swear to God!"

He knelt there and gasped, swallowing hard, large pointed ears twitching front to side to back, sifting through the sounds of the night for the one sound he needed.

What he didn't expect was the shot.

The bullet struck him high on the right shoulder, the force of it nearly toppling him off the rock. He snarled and whirled, glaring up at the ridge, snarled again and slapped at his shoulder where the fire had lodged, a furrow, not a hole, and he growled, tempted to return and teach the cop a lesson.

Another shot, this one thirty yards to his right.

Blind.

Damn, he thought; the stupid kid is firing blind, I don't believe it.

He passed a hand gingerly over the wound,

grimacing at the matted fur, concentrating as he listened to the shouts, the orders, calming himself.

Concentrating.

Dampening the fire.

He could well imagine the conversation above:

I don't see anything.

Down there I saw it.

It?

A big thing you know? I swear it must've been covered in fur. Really hairy, you know what I mean?

Hairy. Big.

I swear!

Sure: sure you do. You just shot a big, hairy thing. right?

Jesus Christ.

Nope, I don't think so.

He came too close to laughing, and clambered swiftly over the rock and continued down, shifting his angle of descent until he was practically directly below the crime scene.

The fire was gone.

The furrow would be, in minutes.

There were no more sounds of possible pursuit. If he had had the time, he would have felt sorry for the poor guy who'd spotted him.

There was no time.

The scent still didn't change, neither weaker nor stronger. The rogue hadn't fled at anything like frightened speed. It was taking its time, confident its human pursuit would never guess what it was, would never believe it had escaped the way it had.

The cries and shouts grew more faint.

The flare of a flashlight couldn't reach this far down.

When he found himself on a narrow ledge, he took a few precious moments to allow his night vision to sharpen further. His arms and legs ached, and trembled slightly from the beating they been taking. His great head swung slowly side to side, snuffling at the air, marking the scent he'd been following.

Below, a pair of cruisers drove slowly southward, spotlights on their roofs attempting to penetrate the slope's trees.

He waited until they passed, looked over the ledge, and jumped before he could talk himself out of it.

Twenty feet, maybe more, before he hit the stony ground, fell to all fours, and launched himself into a sprint as the ground leveled for a while before dropping off again. He had reached the mountain's skirt, and the angle wasn't nearly as sharp as it had been. Movement was easier.

But then, it was for the rogue, too.

He didn't worry about the searchers down here. There were too few of them so far, avoiding them would be easy. What he needed was a direction for the rogue—it seemed as if he had gone straight for the highway, no deviations. Did he have a car down here, waiting? A cave? From what Joanne had told him, the mountain was riddled with them, the largest transformed into tourist attractions.

Fifteen minutes brought him to ground nearly level with the road. He stood well back in the trees, testing the air, catching his breath. Diagonally across the highway, about three hundred yards to his right, were house lights and the vague outline of a split-rail fence. A glance up and over his shoulder, another look at the house, and he figured that must be Nora Costo's place. Another cruiser sped past, followed by a dark-sided van. SWAT team? he wondered, and stepped away from the tree. At that moment what felt like a bomb exploded across the top of his shoulders. He cried out howled as he fell face first to the ground. He couldn't think, couldn't see, and had no chance to protect himself when another explosion killed all the light.

19

. . . blood . . .

Voices:

"Over there."

"What the hell did you . . . Jesus!"

"Well, how was I supposed to know, Sergeant? I heard all the commotion, I go running over, I—"

"Enough, officer, enough."

"What's he doing out here, anyway?"

"FBI."

"Fucking Beanpod Idiot, you mean."

. . . blood . . .

He heard her before he saw her, smelled her before she knelt beside him.

"Oh my God, look at your head."

Tires shrieking on the road, voices in the woods, the deafening slap of a helicopter's rotors.

"Sergeant, you want me to get an ambulance?"

"Good Lord, you didn't call one yet?"

"Thought he was dead. Ain't no hurry if the guy's not breathing."

Richard pushed himself up on one elbow, trying not to scream. "No ambulance."

She leaned closer. "What?"

"No ambulance."

"Sure. And tomorrow, you're gonna walk on water."

Fireflies sparked across his vision, rising from the conflagration rising from his back. With his free hand he braced himself against her knee and rose farther.

"No ambulance."

"Richard, this isn't the movies, honey, you're bashed up, bashed in, and there's no way I'm going to let you die out here."

Christ, he thought, why won't she listen?

He squeezed, and she gasped. "Your car?"

"Right here."

Another push, and he was upright. Swaying. Bits of leaf and twig dangling from his hair, clots of dirt and mud clinging to his jacket.

"The hotel," he said, trying to focus on her face.

"Now that's just plain dumb."

He wanted to yell at her, but the longer he stayed here, the more danger he was in.

"Tell them," he said, gesturing toward the others hovering near the road, "it's not as bad as it looks."

"Richard—"

He glared at her. "Tell them, Jo, tell them it's just a scalp wound and get me out of here."

He saw the rebellion, automatic and justified, but she must have seen something as well, because she stood, gripped his arm, and helped him to his feet.

"Sarge?"

"It's all right. Damn Yankee can't fall down a mountain without scraping his knees, bunking his thick skull on a damn stump."

Someone he couldn't see snickered.

Someone else declared there was movement up the road, haul ass, they needed reinforcements.

"It's all right," Joanne insisted, when the last one hesitated. "You want to miss being in on the kill?"

The patrolman half saluted and took off.

Richard wiped an arm across his eyes, and would have toppled backward if she hadn't kept her grip.

"You will explain."

"Hotel. Hurry."

. . . he could feel the blood . . .

He lay on his side across the back seat, swaying with the car's movement as she raced toward the city. She had put a light blanket over him, covering him to his shoulders. It didn't help much; he couldn't chase the cold.

"You get blood all over my car, Turpin, you clean it up, you understand?"

He grunted.

The fireflies wouldn't leave, the conflagration wouldn't subside. He bit down on his lower lip, one pain for another, but it didn't do any good.

Joanne snapped into the radio, arguing with her lieutenant. She couldn't be in two places at the same time, she told him. Stay at the scene, stay with the FBI, why doesn't he make up his goddamn mind?

For a change there was no static: "Language protocol, Detective."

She apologized flatly, and told him what she had told the others, that Turpin had injured himself a good one, am ambulance would be too slow so she was taking him to the hospital herself.

"How bad is he you got to play nursemaid, Minster?"

"Government, remember?" was all she said. "Your idea, not mine."

Silence and static.

"Drop him off, come right back, Detective."

She acknowledged, dropped the mike on the seat beside her, and glared at the rearview mirror. "If I lose my shield because of this, Turpin, I'll kill you."

He grunted again, not daring to speak, not knowing if he could speak, and not caring about her goddamn shield. He was hurt, and hurt badly, and it wasn't healing the way it should have.

Awkwardly, he reached behind his left ear, touched his hair, then checked his hand in the intermittent light that flowed through the car.

It was thick, barely flowing, but it was still his blood.

He couldn't think.

He didn't understand.

"Hang on, Richard," she said gently. "We're coming up on the bridge. Bumpy ride."

Why the hell was he still bleeding?

The fireflies flared into a solid white wall when the car slammed into a pothole.

. . . he could smell the blood . . .

"Talk to me, Richard," she said quietly and urgently. "Talk to me, don't die on me, talk to me, come on, talk to me."

He began to appreciate the fireflies. At least they were proof he was still alive.

"Talk to me."

"Yes."

He heard the sighed "Thank God."

The car slowed, and he slid toward the door as she swung around a corner.

"How the hell did you get down there so fast?"

He swallowed, his throat feeling as if it were packed with sand. "Flew."

"Not funny."

"Luck."

"Miracle, you mean." A glance over her shoulder. "How'd you get hurt? A tree, rock, what? Keep talking, Richard. Christ, I must be nuts. Momma always said I'd go nuts one of these days, dealing with all the scum of the earth. I'm nuts, that's all there is to it."

The fireflies danced.

"Richard, talk to me, come on, talk to me."

"He . . ." He tried to sit up, but the motion of the car kept him down. "He hit me."

Her voice rose: "You saw him? Jesus, Richard, you saw him?"

He shook his head, and groaned at the explosion that threatened to swamp him. "No," he said. "No. Came from behind me."

His eyes fluttered closed; he saw himself charging like a fool through the trees, following the scent, feeling the explosion, unable to . . .

His eyes snapped open.

Doubled back; the bastard doubled back on his own trail and just stood there, waiting for him.

He knew I was coming.

He groaned again, this time in frustration.

"Richard?"

"How soon?"

"Two minutes. You going to die on me?"

"Nope."

"Then what's this all about?"

"You'll see. Be patient."

Southern and deadly: "Honey, this damn well better be good."

*   *   *

. . . he could taste the blood . . .

He gripped the back of the seat and hauled himself up, bracing himself for the fiery detonation in his skull, the one that mercifully didn't come. His stomach roiled bile into his throat. The fireflies merged with the lights outside as she pulled into the parking entrance, flashed her badge at the attendant who wanted to stop her, and turned sharply left, bringing them down one level. Below ground. Where it was silent.

Once she had stopped, she jumped out and yanked open the back door, suddenly unsure of what to do next.

He half crawled, half slid out to his feet, looked at the ramp and said, "I'll never make it."

She was pale and couldn't keep from staring at his head. But she said nothing. She kept the blanket around his shoulders, hauling it up to cover his neck, and most of the blood; there wasn't much she could do about the blood that matted his hair. An arm slipped around his waist, an order to lean on her, she was stronger than she looked, and they began the upward climb.

"You're drunk," she whispered when they came out at street level.

He didn't need to act. His legs weren't working, the fireflies were blinding him, and the throbbing in his head trebled every noise and deafened him. He stared at the ground, then at the carpet, seeing feet pass him, hearing some disgust, some giggles, someone ask if the little lady could use some help with her friend.

The little lady declined. Politely.

Richard would have laughed had he had the strength.

At the elevators she showed her badge again, clearing everyone out. When a pair of pointy silver boots complained bitterly, she suggested he talk to the management. Not very politely this time, and the doors closed.

"You're not gonna die, right?"

He stared at the floor, and said nothing. Right now, there was nothing he could say to chase the fear in her voice. He had to concentrate on standing up, concentrate on walking when they reached the third floor, concentrate on not screaming when she leaned him too heavily against the wall and searched him for the key card to let them inside.

"The bed," she said when the door closed behind them.

"No." He pushed her gently toward the couch. "Sit down."

"But—"

"Sit down. This'll take a few minutes, but . . . just sit, Jo, just sit."

He made his way into the other room without falling, used the bed to help him keep his feet, and tried not to stumble when he entered the bathroom. Before he turned on the light, he looked out and saw her, on the couch but sitting forward, trying to see him through the dark.

"Don't leave," he said hoarsely, and closed the door, turned on the light, looked in the mirror over the small porcelain sink.

He knew then, and raised a weak fist.

Silver; the son of a bitch had hit him with something heavily laced with silver.

"So why aren't you dead?" he asked his reflection. "Why didn't he finish it?"

He grabbed the edge of the basin with both hands, lowered his head, and closed his eyes.

The shift was agony.

He confined it to his head and shoulders as best he could, and didn't look up, didn't want to look up, just waited until all the fireflies died and the conflagration died and he could think again without wishing he were dead.

. . . blood . . .

. . . on the jaws of Anubis . . .

Stiffly, moving an inch at a time, he stripped off his jacket and shirt, splashed cold water on his face, and grimaced at the blood and woodland filth that swirled down the drain. It took the face cloth and two hand towels before the water ran reasonably clear; then he washed again, and stripped to his shorts.

He was still dizzy, could still barely walk. He needed to rest, needed sleep. The rogue was out there—and close, so damn close—but the way he felt now, he wouldn't be able to fight his own shadow.

Maybe Poulard was right; maybe he was getting too old for this job. If that second blow had hit his head instead of his shoulders . . .

He turned off the light and opened the door.

Joanne was on her feet in the middle of the sitting room, a single lamp burning behind her. "I thought . . . I was going to come in. I thought—"

He pulled back the quilt and blanket, and slipped under the sheet, with a slight groan not entirely just for her benefit.

She took a step closer. "I'll get a doctor now, okay?"

"No," he said weakly. "I'm all right. Like you said to that cop, it looked worse than it was. Cold water does wonders, believe it or not."

She came into the room then and stood by the footboard. "This is nuts. You need a doctor. You need stitches. Damn, Turpin, you practically fell down a goddamn mountain, then got yourself nailed by a killer."

"I'll be all right," he insisted gamely, and added with a smile, "If it'll make you feel any better, I'm going to feel like hell in the morning." He laughed tightly. "Hell, I feel like hell now."

"This makes no sense."

He could feel himself slipping away, down where the healing was. He wanted to say something to her, to ease the concern so clear in her voice, to clear the fear for him he could see in her eyes.

All he could do was sigh.

"I can't stay," she said suddenly, sidling toward the sitting room.

"I know."

"He'll kill me. And that—"

"You'll catch him."

Her laugh was bitter. "Yeah. Right. Like I'm Superwoman or something, huh?" Angrily she snatched up her coat, switched off the lamps, and grabbed for the doorknob. "Maybe I'll stop by later."

"Thanks, but you'll be working all night."

A shrug.

"Jo?"

The door was open, light slipping into the room. She looked at him, frowning because she couldn't see anything but a vague lump in the bed.

"You are, you know."

"What?"

"Super."

Did she blush? He couldn't tell because she was gone too quickly, and his vision was as well. There were no fireflies, but there was a insistent dull throbbing, and a faint burning across his shoulders that forced him to lie on his stomach, hands buried under the pillow.

He would heal, but he'd been lucky.

Right now he was furious at himself, for running

off like that, for letting the damn rogue catch him in such an amateur trap, and for wishing Jo didn't take her job so seriously.

He closed his eyes and waited, groaned and got up, chained and bolted the door, and returned to bed.

Still angry.

Still aching.

Until the healing dark took him, and all he could see was his own blood.

20

Blanchard sat in his room, alone, darkness relieved only by the light that seeped around the edges of the draperies.

In his right hand he held a half-empty tumbler of Southern Comfort, while his left dangled motionless over the arm of the chair. The only time he moved was when he heard a burst of activity outside his door. Whatever passed for an evening's entertainment at this place must have begun, and he had a feeling it would last most of the night.

There was no temptation to wander the hotel, to visit any of the dozen parties announced in garish flyers taped to the walls.

Once he had seen Turpin and the lady cop hurry out of the building, once his flare-up at Strand had subsided, he had retreated here. To calm down. To consider.

After an hour he turned on the television and flicked through the channels, shaking his head in disgust until the bulletins had started.

Another killing on the mountain, just as brutal as the others. Police from two states were out in force, an immediate curfew had been clamped onto the city, and more information would be delivered as it was received.

The television went off when it obvious the local news had nothing but pissant speculation and rehashed history to give its viewers.

He sipped.

He considered driving out there just to see what was really going on, and discarded the notion instantly. The rogue was gone; and the odds of finding Turpin alone were too long to take the chance. The man would probably be out there until dawn.

The fingers of his left hand twitched.

He sipped, letting the single ice cube settle briefly against his teeth.

His problem now wasn't really a problem at all: normally, he would have found a way to confuse the issue, as he had usually done before, not bothering with the rogue because, in the long run, it didn't matter to him one way or the other. Once the waters had been muddied, his job was over.

But that was normally.

Now he had to decide if the rogue really didn't matter. Crimmins the Prick would probably tell him that they both had to go, the rogue and Turpin. The rogue, because capture by others would surely rend the Veil, and Crimmins and his people didn't seem ready to let it go that far yet; Turpin, because simple capture was out of the question.

He sipped.

Normally, others came in after him and took care of the rogue, made it vanish or whatever, and whatever Crimmins did with it was his business, not Blanchard's. Unless there were too many killings, which generally caught the Warders' attention. Those he stayed away from; those brought Turpin, and normally, he didn't want anything to do with the Strider.

But that was normally.

Crimmins had stepped over the line, both here and in San Francisco.

"Ignorant little man, my ass," he muttered into the tumbler.

Then he thought about Wanda Strand, and his left hand became a fist.

He woke up with a silent cry, and to sweat drenching his hair and pillow, blanket and sheet tangled and shoved to the foot of the bed.

A second passed before he remembered where he was, and another before he realized something wasn't right, that he hadn't been dreaming.

Until he felt the pain that shouldn't have been.

It wasn't all that bad, he'd felt worse, much worse, but the fact was, he shouldn't have been feeling any pain at all.

He should have been healing, and he wasn't.

Slowly, almost holding his breath, he swung his legs over the side and sat up, slumping, waiting for his mind to clear, passing a hand over his face and back through his hair.

"Damn," he whispered. "Damn."

He straightened and rolled his shoulders, and the pain slammed him back onto the mattress, legs jerking uncontrollably, fists tucked tightly under his chin, arms pressed to his ribs as if they could squeeze the pain out.

He waited for it to pass.

It didn't.

"It's quite easy, you see," Marcus Spiro explained as if imparting a great secret, "to let all this go to your head. I've seen it a hundred . . . no, a thousand times in a thousand cities. A few autographs, a few speeches, and the less disciplined begin to believe that they're special." He leaned over the table. "That they're actually somebody if you know what I mean."

Wanda nodded solemnly, letting her fingers caress the stem of her wine glass slowly.

"Not that I wasn't immune in the beginning myself," the writer admitted with a sad smile of self-deprecation. "I rather enjoyed the fuss, don't you see. In many ways, in those days, it validated all the sacrifices one makes when one has to work at such a truly lonely occupation."

She nodded again, staring at her fingers, once in a while shifting her gaze to his face, to prove that she was listening.

He sat back and sighed, unbuttoning his tweed jacket as if it were too tight across his middle. "I know better now, of course."

"Of course," she said. "With age comes wisdom."

"Exactly." He chuckled, tilted his head. "And foolishness, too, I fear, my dear. Because every so often, when I am feted at one of these outlandish conventions, I allow myself to taken along for the ride. Caution to the wind and all that, you see."

"Why not? You work hard, so you ought to be able to kick up your heels once in a while." She ducked her head and smiled. "You must clear out the brain cells while letting your ego have its day."

He smiled expansively. "Absolutely! Absolutely!"

The restaurant was nearly empty. Only a handful of people sat in the booths. A lull, she thought. It was just past nine; in a while there would probably be a rush to beat last call. She looked around Spiro, down the length of the room. All right, a dribble. It'll fill up, but it won't get hectic.

"You know, my dear Ms. Strand," Spiro said, keeping his voice low, "I am surprised, quite frankly, to find someone not a part of this circus who actually seems to understand what it's like. Being someone like me, I mean to say."

A waitress brought them another round without having to be asked, followed by a tall, bearded man, who came up to the railing and, after an apologetic glance at her, tapped Spiro on the shoulder.

"Ah, Leon!" A hand waved vaguely. "Leon, please make sure this young lady gets a medal, won't you? She has graciously allowed me to intrude on her solitude for the past hour, and bore her to silent tears."

Wanda nodded politely at the newcomer, who couldn't quite meet her eyes, and for no reason at all, she found that charming. Nevertheless, as she drank, a faint disturbing chill made her check the window, thinking that perhaps it might have started snowing.

"Mr. Spiro," Hendean said deferentially, "will you need me anymore tonight?"

Spiro shook his head. "Of course not, Leon. I'm going to get a little more drunk, check a party or two, and retire early. It's been a long day."

"Okay. Thanks. Do you want a wake-up call or anything? Room service breakfast?"

"God, no!" Spiro shuddered dramatically. "I have a panel at eleven, I think. I'll be there, don't worry."

The two men conversed quietly, and Wanda looked away, toward the lobby door. Bored was absolutely the right word. Spiro had invited himself to her table, and she'd been too distracted to discourage him. By the time she realized what a monumental bore he was, news of the latest murder was on the large-screen TV down by the bar, and she didn't want to move, didn't want to miss a thing.

It was easy to split her attention between the news and the writer; all Spiro required was a nod and smile now and then—his ego took care of the rest.

"My dear?"

She blinked, smiling automatically as she rubbed one arm against the persistent chill. Leon was gone, and Spiro had changed. His dark eyes were bright, his posture more relaxed, and she groaned silently when he damn near winked as he suggested that they retire to his room with a few of his close friends. A private party. Intelligent conversation. Wit and repartee. Surely, he said, she would find that more stimulating than sitting alone in a bar.

He leaned closer, and she leaned away without thinking.

He's on something, she thought then. His eyes, the way he tilted his head, the way his tongue touched his lips, not really moistening them.

Without reason, he made her nervous.

And when he repeated the invitation, all she could think of was, *come into my parlor said the spider to the fly*.

There was no telling how much time had passed before the pain subsided.

He breathed with open mouth, tasting the salt from tears and sweat, blinking in the dark. trying to see.

"Damn."

It was as if someone had stabbed him with an ice pick between his shoulder blades. And kept it there, every so often pushing it in a little.

He tried to reach the spot with one hand, then both, but all he succeeded in doing was push his face deeper into the pillow, and threaten a cramp in his legs. When he tried to get up onto his forearms and knees, the pain shoved him back again.

"Jo," he whispered.

No one answered.

Blanchard set the empty tumbler on the night table and pushed himself out the chair.

He couldn't sit here any longer.

He switched on the television in case there was any late news he needed to know, and went into the bathroom. Once his vision adjusted to the overhead light, he opened the kit and checked himself in the mirror.

It had occurred to him that maybe Turpin didn't have to be on Lookout Mountain until dawn. That maybe muddying the waters was exactly what was needed. If for no other reason that to piss Crimmins off.

He grinned.

Time, he decided, to do his job.

So he steadied himself, reached up, and began to take off his face.

Spiro was visibly disappointed when she declined his invitation, but he was nevertheless gracious about it. A murmured apology for taking up so much of her time, a slightly drunken bow, and he was gone, immediately latched onto by a handful of younger people, who followed him chattering out of the room.

Wanda stared at her glass, only vaguely aware that he had left.

There was a quiver to her left hand.

Her right gripped the stem lightly with the pads of her fingers.

The chill had begun to fade, but there was no mistaking it. None.

She had never pretended to be anything else than what she was—a paid assassin whose credentials were inarguable, and whose loyalty could be counted on. She had few skills in diplomacy, fewer in politics, and paid no attention to whatever subtleties Crimmins tried to attach to her job.

She didn't much care.

She killed. Simple as that.

Like this job. A last-minute thing, a phone call in the middle of the night that had rousted her from bed so she could listen to Crimmins vent his rage and demand retribution for damn near an hour. When she had finally calmed him down, he told her what he wanted.

Nothing fancy, nothing cute.

Just make damn sure Miles Blanchard didn't leave Chattanooga alive.

She was surprised, but she didn't ask questions. Blanchard was a walking ego trip, and from the first time they had met, she had had a feeling Crimmins and his people weren't going to carry him forever.

She hadn't counted on this, however; she hadn't counted on being able to locate a rogue without half trying.

It almost made her laugh aloud; instead, she gripped the stem more tightly.

Blanchard, the son of a bitch, had once laughingly called her a Seer because of her hunches, most of which were right when it came to hunting the Garou. She didn't really believe it, mainly because she had never been able to summon the skill—if that's what it was—at will. Didn't believe, that is, until it happened. Even then she didn't waste time trying to figure it out.

It happened.

It was right.

Almost always, someone died.

She felt the chill deepen briefly, bone-deep and dry, before it faded completely, and knew it wasn't from the weather outside.

Once she realized that, she realized something else—that she actually might know who it was.

All right, he thought, accepting momentary defeat; all right, it's all right.

He lay on his stomach, arms at his sides, and stared blindly toward the sitting room. Movement brought the pain, so he didn't move. All he had to do was wait. Sooner or later, Jo would be back. He suspected with a smile she wasn't being terribly effective out there tonight, not after what she had seen happen to him, and she would take the first opportunity to get away.

When she did, when she returned, he would have her check his back, to find what had to be a sliver of silver still lodged there, and get it out somehow. It was the only explanation. Nothing else would cause him this much agony.

All he had to do was wait.

Which he did until he remembered that he'd latched and bolted the door. Even if she came back, she wouldn't be able to get in.

All right, then, he thought, you have no choice.

He moved, and cried out softly, and moved, and tasted the bile, and finally collapsed back onto the bed, sweating through the chills that stiffened his muscles.

All he had to do now was wait.

There was nothing else he could do.

He was dying.

Wanda emptied her glass in a single, long swallow, and declined the waitress' offer of a refill. The restaurant/bar was empty save for a couple in a booth midway along. There was basketball on the television. A check proved the lobby was deserted.

She leaned back and pulled the ivory wand from her pocket, keeping it below the table's edge. Pressing a hidden button snapped out a blade made of silver, serrated and barbed. She lay it across one palm, then drew it back and forth as if sharpening it on her skin.

The big man or the writer?

One of them was Garou.

Annoyed with herself now for not recognizing it sooner, she folded the blade back into the ivory, snapped it out, folded it in, over and over, while she sorted the possibilities and the options.

Ten minutes later the weapon was back in her pocket, and she was on her feet.

Realistically, there were no options, at least not for tonight. The argument with Blanchard had sent her to the bar, to the wine, and her reflexes weren't nearly as sharp as they ought to be. Her right hand touched the back of her head absently, and she hissed silently when she felt the small bump hitting the wall had caused. Even if Blanchard hadn't been her primary objective, that shove would have made him so, no matter what Crimmins thought.

Now she had two targets.

The payment wouldn't increase, but that was all right.

From all she had gathered, Blanchard, when he had to, killed coldly, without emotion.

Wanda, when it happened, made sure it was fun.

She made her way to the exit, touching booths and chairs as she walked to keep her balance grounded. The lights were bright, the noise outside loud, and she hoped she could make it back to the room without falling over. Once there, and once sleep had gotten rid of the effects of the wine, she would figure out when and where the best times would be.

It didn't take that long.

She spotted an easel set between the elevator doors, holding a placard announcing the next day's big event at the convention: an evening-long masquerade that would culminate in a huge party in the ballroom upstairs.

She grinned, and turned to a man waiting beside her, black hair, skin-tight jump suit, enough rhinestones and bangles to blind the blind. Pointy ears. "Who are you supposed to be?" she asked, wide-eyed, Southern belle.

The man smiled shyly. "Vulcan Elvis."

Oh my God, she thought, this is gonna be a snap.

In the last hour before dawn, a slow wind rising outside the window, Richard opened his eyes and smelled the blood. His blood.

21

She was gliding.

The wind held her above the mountain, cried in her ears, made her eyes water. It was terrifying, and it was great, and she couldn't stop herself from yelling aloud.

She was gliding.

Below was mostly brown and tan, with smudges of green where the pines muscled in. Winks and flares of light from reflections off glass, off the roofs of cars, off the river that tucked the city into its bend.

She was flying.

Listening to the wind and to the flutter of the air-foil and to the creak of the frame and to the groan of her arms as they steered her slowly, then rapidly down the side of the mountain.

Up here she had no troubles; up here the only shooting she did was along a current that wanted to take her away. No place special.

Just . . . away.

The problem was down there.

In the trees she could see something pacing her, something large and black, and she knew it wasn't a

bear and she knew it wasn't a panther and she knew
that the lieutenant's face had no business being at
her right shoulder.

"Hey!" he called. "Hey, Minster!"

Go away, she thought; damn it, I'm flying.

He grabbed her shoulder and shook it gently.

Jesus, she nearly yelled; are you trying to kill me?

"Hey." Gently now. "Hey, Joanne."

She blinked, blinked again, and she was in the
passenger seat of her car, no longer flying, grounded
in front of the Chestnut Street bus station. Rubbing
her eyes with her knuckles, she swung her legs
around when he opened the door.

She tried to focus on her watch, shivering so hard
her teeth almost chattered. "Damn. What time is it?"

He squinted at the sky. "If it weren't for the
clouds, it'd be a bit past dawn. Come on, wake up."

It came back to her in wisps: a call, another killing,
this time a washed-out hooker named Nina Sue Losi,
a regular around here, discovered by a half-stoned
friend at the back of the narrow parking lot between
the station and the hotel next door. Millson had
grabbed Joanne and a few others, and they'd made a
screaming convoy into the city. Too late, as usual,
but not too late to see the slices the killer had taken
out of the woman before he had dumped her.

No one had seen a thing.

"Hey."

"I'm awake, I'm awake. Jeez, Lieutenant, gimmie a
break."

He grinned, wiped a gloved hand under his nose,
and straightened. "No sense sticking around. I got
the boys on it now."

She nodded.

More wisps: it hadn't taken them long to see that
this wasn't the Task Force beast. Although the

wounds were similar, there hadn't been anything missing. Nina Sue was all there. What was left of her, that is, sprawled in all her blood.

Once Millson understood that, he called in the regular Homicide crew, asking her to wait in the car until they arrived.

She scratched vigorously through her hair, eased out of the car, and stretched. The wind had died down, but the clouds remained. She sniffed the sharp air and cursed—there'd be snow before long. Just what they needed. Hell, for this kind of weather she might as well be living in Chicago.

Crime ribbons rippled; lights flashed; a patrolman stood on the pavement, keeping a crowd of hotel guests away from the area. A TV van parked nose-in a few feet away, a weary reporter standing with a mike in a wash of vivid light.

Joanne yawned so hard her jaw popped, and Millson laughed.

"Go away," he told her with mock severity. "Sleep in a real bed for a couple of hours for a change, be back at the office by noon." He gestured toward the street. "The others are already gone." He took a step away and turned. "Forget the office. Be sure that Fed hasn't died while we were playing first. Then come in."

"But—"

"Joanne," he said, exhaustion making his voice hoarse and his face haggard, "we didn't find anything out there, and we sure ain't gonna do it walking around like zombies."

He turned his back, and she decided not to argue. A muttered "thanks," and she slipped back inside, closed the door, and squirmed across the seat behind the wheel. The car was frigid, the windshield already beginning to fog over, and it took three tries before the engine fired.

A real bed sounded real good about now, but she couldn't help thinking about Richard. That blood. She rubbed her eyes again, slapped herself gently on her cheeks, and decided it wouldn't hurt to do what the lieutenant had asked. The Read House was only a few blocks away. A finger touched her jacket's breast pocket, making sure she still had the room key. A look in, that's all. Get him something if he needed it.

That all? she asked sarcastically as she pulled away from the curb; you sure that's the only reason?

The streets were still, only a few cars moving, no one on the sidewalks at all. She pulled into the parking entrance, straight into an area marked off by orange traffic cones, directly in front of the entrance.

"Hey," the attendant called. "Hey, lady, that's reserved. You can't—"

"Oh, yes, I can," she answered brightly, holding up her badge. "Thanks," and she was inside before he could say another word.

The building was eerily quiet.

A coatless bellman vacuumed the lobby carpet. There were no clerks behind the counter. A teenager in a fatigue jacket slumped in one of the couches, reading a paperback book.

Joanne held her jacket closed with one hand, feeling a slight chill that didn't leave her until the elevator let her off on the third floor.

Silence, still.

Despite the carpeting, it seemed as if her footfalls echoed.

When she stood in front of Turpin's door, key card in her hand, she hesitated. Yes, he was hurt; no, she wasn't his nursemaid. Yes, he was a grown man; no, she had a murderer to catch, and baby-sitting wasn't part of the investigation.

Yes; no.

The faint ring of the elevator bell made her jump and look guiltily around.

Damn it, she thought. She inserted the card and entered the room quickly, closing the door while she waited for her vision to adjust to the gloom.

He was still in bed, but the covers had somehow landed down around his ankles, and she could see a dark stain in the middle of his back.

He stirred, and groaned.

Oh my God, she thought, and hurried around the bed, looked down, and gasped aloud.

"Jo?"

Blood on his back, some of it dried to a crust, some of it fresh.

"Jo?"

"Yes, it's me." She knelt beside him, a hand hovering over the wound. "I thought you were . . . you said . . ."

With great effort he turned his face on the pillow, and she swallowed heavily. His face was drawn, old, eyes retreating deep into their sockets, cheeks gouged with hollows.

He managed a smile. "You came."

"Lieutenant's orders."

His lips quivered. "I need help."

"I can see that. I'll call the ambulance."

"No!" He tried to reach for her arm, but she could see the agony that stopped him. "My . . . my back," he said weakly. "In my back."

She could see nothing when she looked, and hoped her fear wasn't evident as she yanked open the drapes by the headboard, then turned on all the lights, discarding her coat as she did. The bathroom door was wide open; she switched on that light as well, soaked a face cloth in cold water, and knelt by the bed again.

"It's going to hurt," he said, lips pulled taut over his teeth. "Don't stop."

As quickly and tenderly as she could, she cleaned the blood from his back, circling around a small black smudge between his shoulder blades. He was rigid, and she was angry for not listening to herself, for not fetching a doctor, for not resisting the plea in his voice, however weak it may be.

"What . . . what do you see?"

She leaned close, damning the inadequate light, tilting her head until . . . "It . . . damn, Richard, it looks like some kind of splinter. A big one."

"Get it out."

Trembling and unsure, she tried to pinch the slippery protrusion between her fingers, but they couldn't do it, and his muffled cry rocked her back on her heels. She flapped her hands helplessly. "I can't."

"The knife."

"What?"

"You have that knife?"

None of it made sense. What the hell did he want with her knife? Dig that thing out? She fumbled in her pockets until she brought it out, stared at it stupidly until, with a silly grin, she remembered the tweezers.

"If you have to dig," he said weakly, "do it."

"Richard, I am not going to—"

He did grab her arm then, and yanked her off-balance until their noses nearly touched. "I'm dying, Jo. It's not just a splinter. It's killing me. For Christ's sake, if you have to, *dig the damn thing out.*"

His eyes closed before she could react, his hand releasing her, his arm flopping over the edge of the mattress.

He's crazy, she thought; hell, I'm crazy.

Blood rose in droplets around the splinter.

When she touched his shoulder, it was cold; when she touched his brow, it was clammy; and it took a few seconds before she could see him breathing.

Poison, she realized; that thing is poisoned.

She rinsed the face cloth, grabbed a hand towel, and took a number of deep breaths to steady herself.

Crazy.

The tweezers were tiny, holding them was awkward, and she had to squint to see the end of the splinter.

She whispered, "Okay, here we go," and settled the tweezers as far down the splinter's shaft as she could without actually pinching it. But as soon she did it, he bucked, startling her and throwing her backward.

"Jesus!"

Blood in droplets, flowing freely.

A vague darkening of the rest of his skin.

Aw, Jesus, she thought, pushed her hair back, and tried again, this time pressing the heel of her left hand against his spine.

When the tweezers pinched, he bucked again, but she was ready and held him down while she pulled sharply, feeling the splinter give but not come free. She cursed, dried her palms on her jeans, and tried again. Again there was movement, yet still she couldn't work it loose.

Please, she thought; please, don't make me dig for it, God, I don't want to do that.

The third attempt failed when she couldn't stop her hand from trembling.

Richard sighed, a long bubbling sound that made her close her eyes until it stopped.

You shot a kid, you can't pull out a goddamn splinter?

This is different.

"One more time," she said, "and then I'm getting a doctor, I don't care what you say."

He didn't answer, and she came close to panic, trying to find a pulse in his neck, nearly sagging in relief when she did, and nearly giving up, the hell with him, this was all just too damn weird.

Her hand steadied.

She pressed down on his spine, just below the splinter.

She held her breath, pinched the tweezers, and this time didn't try to yank it, just pull it, pausing when she felt the grip slipping, ignoring the flesh rippling beneath her, staring only at the blood and the splinter and seeing nothing but the tweezers as they gripped and pulled, so slowly she wanted to scream.

"Come on." She glared at it. "Come on, you stupid . . . son of a . . . bitch!"

So intent on the task was she, that when the splinter slid out of Richard's back, she didn't realize she had it until she saw the empty hole, much wider than it should be, welling with fresh blood. Then she stared at the tweezers, blinking, grinning, the grin fading when she saw the splinter's length.

Not a splinter, she thought; damn, that's no splinter.

It was a good three inches long, and when she held it close to her face, she knew it wasn't wood.

"Richard?"

He didn't move.

She swabbed his back with the cloth.

"Richard?"

His body shuddered violently.

"That's it." She pushed shakily to her feet. "That's it. I'm getting—"

"No."

She almost didn't hear him.

"No."

Her mouth opened, closed, and she stomped into the bathroom, threw the cloth into the basin, and took only a second to stare at the bloody towels lying in a heap in the corner, before she looked in the mirror. "You are an idiot," she told her reflection.

"Jo."

She turned.

His eyes were open, mouth parted in a crooked smile.

Green eyes.

Green fire.

"Stay," he asked, and the Green fire vanished.

She said nothing. Carefully she placed the splinter, blade, spike, whatever the hell it was, on a narrow shelf beneath the mirror, rinsed the cloth, and took it back into the bedroom.

There she washed his back again, felt his brow, and it was warm.

Then she looked at the place where the splinter had been.

"Oh."

The hole was gone.

22

Just before noon, the snow began to fall.

Small flakes mixed with large, not enough wind to make them all dance.

The city was convinced that it wouldn't last long. It seldom did. When it snowed.

Richard woke with a start, a loud grunt, and sat up. And tensed when he remembered the fire in his back. But it was gone, and he relaxed, tempted to slump back and sleep a little more.

"Richard, you okay?"

He looked to his right. Joanne stood nervously in the center of the other room, looking small in the gray light that came through the window. "Yes," he said at last. "Thanks to you, yes."

He could smell the fear, and the undirected anger.

"You owe me," she told him, trying to be firm. "You promised me an explanation." She shook her head. "You owe me big time. Now."

He didn't bother to argue; she was right. He flung the covers aside and, ignoring his nakedness, strode to the armoire to fetch a clean pair of jeans from the top drawer. As he pulled them on, he debated how much to say, how much she could receive before she couldn't take anymore. He pulled up the zipper, fixed the brass button, and used his hands to comb back his hair.

"Talk to me," she said, just shy of imploring. "Please." An impatient gesture toward the telephone. "I have to be at headquarters soon."

He moved to the archway, watching as she put the coffee table between them. Doing his best not to smile, he pointed at the couch. "Sit down, Jo, please. There's a story I have to tell you. "

He came out of the bathroom with his old face back on. The bloody clothes he had worn were already resting at the bottom of the river, and the hot shower had taken care of the rest. He didn't think the cops would be fooled for very long, but it would make Turpin wonder, maybe confuse him a little.

The telephone rang.

He glared at it, ignored it, and when it stopped, he rubbed his stomach and decided it was time to eat.

The telephone rang.

He knew who it was. What surprised him was how suddenly nervous he was. All that brave talk yesterday, all that anger in California—bluster, nothing but bluster.

If I don't answer, he'll get Strand to find out what's the matter. If not her, then someone else. Lots of them.

The Man of a Thousand Faces would have nowhere to hide.

He grabbed the scrambler from the closet, hooked it up, and waited.

When the telephone rang again, he cleared his throat and lifted the receiver.

"Mr. Blanchard."

Carefully neutral, a hint of his old arrogance: "Yes."

"Are we rested now, Mr. Blanchard? Are we more levelheaded today?"

He took a chance: "I don't know, sir. Are we?"

The pause gave him time to sit on the bed, light a cigarette, stare at the snow slapping wetly against his window.

"There are pressures, Mr. Blanchard, most of which you'll never understand. If you're lucky."

It was as close to an apology as he would ever get. He didn't push it, nor did he gloat. "And on this end, too, sir. Absolutely."

Another pause until: "There's been a slight alteration in the overall campaign."

"I just want to know—you didn't hypnotize me or something like that, right?"

"No."

"I mean, I saw what happened to you, right? It wasn't the lights or anything. Up there." She pointed at the window over her shoulder. "And here. This morning. I saw it. I saw the blood."

"Yes."

She shook her head. "Impossible. It's a trick."

He pulled the coffee-table back, giving him enough room to sit on its edge without getting too close. He held out a hand. "Let me have the knife."

"Sure." She reached into her jeans and pulled it out.

He took it without comment, opened a blade, and stared at her while he draw a line down his forearm.

"Jesus Christ!"

"Watch," he said. "Watch."

*　　　*　　　*

"Alteration?"

"Addition, rather."

"I don't get it." He was feeling much better. Crimmins sounded like his old pompous-ass self. "What are you talking about?"

"The Strider, Mr. Blanchard."

"Yeah, yeah, I know. I thought you wanted to wait until tomorrow, just before I left."

"That's not the alteration. Not all of it."

Blanchard scowled. This whole thing was getting too bizarre. First, he's threatened if he doesn't take care of Turpin and the rogue, then he's screamed at, now he's told the rules are being changed. Whatever the old fart was up to, Blanchard wished he'd stop playing games and for change be straight with him.

"Are you in position?"

Blanchard nodded. "Yes, sir. Just name the time."

"Tonight."

He shrugged. "No sweat. That it?"

"Not quite, Mr. Blanchard. Not quite."

Richard wanted to take her hand and stroke it, stroke her cheek, stroke her brow. He wanted to take the confusion and the fear from her eyes and from the way her lips struggled not to tremble.

He couldn't.

"It's not a trick, is it," she said, unable to take her gaze from the unblemished arm, or from the blood that had dripped into the handkerchief he had held under the cut.

He shifted.

She shied away to the corner of the couch.

"No. Not a trick."

A hand rose and fell helplessly in her lap, and she looked at the ceiling, out the window, at the ceiling again. She seemed to have a hard time breathing, a hard time focusing. "You going to tell me you're one of those cyborg things? Androids? You know, people that are part machine?"

"No." He smiled. "Nothing like that."

"But—"

"The story," he reminded her. "Let me tell you a story."

She pulled up her legs and wrapped her arms around her shins. "I don't think I want to hear it."

"It's too late, Jo. I'm really sorry, but it's too late. You have to know."

"Look," Blanchard said, feeling his temper slip again, "you want me to take care of Turpin, I can do that. You want me to do it tonight, I can do that, too. What the hell else is there? Sir. The rogue?"

"No. Forget it."

"Then what? Strand?"

"Partly."

He had a hard time not yelling. "Partly what?"

"The Veil, Mr. Blanchard."

"Garou," Richard said. And once it was said, he felt both relieved and fearful. There was only one way to prove the story he would tell, and if it failed, he didn't want to think about what he would have to do.

"Garou?" Jo pushed a nervous hand back through her hair. "I've heard of that. Loup-garou, right? Louisiana? Werewolves or something." She laughed, stopped when he didn't join her. "Oh sure. Right. Lord, how many kinds of fool do you take me for, Turpin?"

"None at all, dahlin'," he said, gently mocking her accent. He stood and returned to the bedroom, searching for the clothes he had worn last night. He found them in the bathroom, in a pile with the bloody towels. He picked up the jeans and took out the cloth sack. Pressed it to his forehead. Inhaled slowly.

When he returned to the sitting room, he swung a chair away from the table, sat, and untied the emerald thread that held the sack closed. He spread it open on the coffee table, and took out the black figure. Held it up between two fingers.

"I know that thing," she said, leaning forward, squinting, interested in spite of herself.

"Anubis."

"Yeah. Right. Egyptian god."

He nodded.

Sarcastically: "That's you?"

He straightened slowly, rose slowly, and moved until the table was between them. "I don't have much time. No time at all."

"Richard, are you all right? I mean, that was a hell of a fall you took."

She had begun her retreat; he couldn't wait any longer.

"Egypt," he told her. "My people, my tribe, came out of Egypt."

Blanchard rolled his eyes, looked heavenward for a large dose of patience. "Okay, the Veil. What about it?"

"It's the way you kill Turpin, Mr. Blanchard."

He scratched the back of his head, hard. "What do you mean? I don't get it."

*　　*　　*

"All of us, all the tribes of the Garou, spend our lives trying to save Gaia. The Earth. There are forces that work against us, not all of them human. But we try, Jo. We keep on trying."

"You rip it, Mr. Blanchard."

He sat up sharply. "I *what*?"

"No secrets anymore, do you understand? No secrets. Their safe time is over."

He didn't like the way the snow sounded like tiny claws on the pane; he didn't like the way the snow blurred the view and turned daylight to gray; he didn't like the way his throat abruptly dried.

"No offense, Mr. Crimmins, but do you know what the hell you're saying here?"

"I know precisely what I'm saying, Mr. Blanchard. I've given it more thought than you'll ever know."

"Jesus." He inhaled slowly. "Jesus H. Christ."

"What separates us from you is something we call the Veil. I am sworn to protect it, as well."

"Can I have a minute here?"

"Take your time, Mr. Blanchard, take your time. I want no misunderstandings."

He placed the receiver carefully on the bed, rose, and walked to the window. There was nothing to see except for the snow, for the struggling traffic, but when he placed his fingertips against the pane, the cold felt damn good.

They were nuts.

Those guys were fucking nuts.

Rip the goddamn Veil?

He made a small noise in his throat, covered his mouth with one hand, and looked over his shoulder at the bed.

Were they out of their goddamn minds?

Christ, this wasn't just some war they would start. This was goddamn Armageddon.

"Your rogue, Jo, is a Garou. That's why you've never found him. You started out looking for an animal, now you're hunting a human. You should have been looking for both."

He couldn't tell a thing from her expression; he couldn't tell how deep her retreat had taken her.

"It's a hunger born of madness. We all . . ." He faltered, looked away, decided to concentrate on the window and the leafless branches outside. "We all must kill to eat. To live. It's a part of us, there's no getting around it, and we . . . I make no excuses for it. The madness is just . . . killing. For the hell of it. For the pleasure of it.

"And my job is to stop it."

"You're crazy," she whispered. "We're both crazy."

"I am a Silent Strider. A loner. Always alone." The wind caused the branches to quiver. Shadows darted across the pane like smears of black rain. "And I am one of the best at what I do."

"Tell that to Curly Guestin."

He glanced at her, pleased—for just that split second, she had taken his word. Right now, it was enough.

"So tell me," she said, shuddering a deep breath, "are you like in the movies? Full moon? Silver bullets? A normal guy one minute, a wolf the next? Fangs and claws, all that shit?"

The bravado and derision were back.

"You'll see."

*   *   *

He picked up the receiver, but he didn't sit down.

"Back, Mr. Crimmins."

"Good."

"So let me get this straight: You still want me to take care of Turpin, but you want me to do it so these people will know what he is?"

"Yes."

"Tonight?"

"Yes."

"And then what?"

There was no answer.

She refused to allow him to touch her, but did as she was bidden when asked to take his place by the coffee-table, her back to him. Then he closed the drapes in both rooms, turned out all the lamps but one.

"Look at the wall, Jo."

She folded her arms under her breasts and scowled. "Some kind of game?"

"Trust me, Jo—"

"Ha."

"—it's better this way."

His shadow rose on the wall by the door.

"You do rabbits and birds?"

"Watch."

"Mr. Crimmins, once I do this thing, then what?"

The shadow began to change.

*   *   *

"You run, Mr. Blanchard."

The shadow grew. Expanded. "That's pretty good," Joanne said. The shadow began to *shift*.

"You run as far away as you can."

He knew what she saw, spreading toward the ceiling:
    The muzzle, the ears, the extended arm and the claws.
    Anubis.
    He heard the whimper, saw her spine grow rigid, and saw her head begin to move.
    "No," he cautioned. Voice deeper. Much deeper. As quiet as it was, it filled the room with its power. "Not unless you really want to know."
    "Trick."
    "No."
    She turned, and she saw him.
    "Oh, Lord," she said, and sat down hard on the floor. "Aw, Jesus."

Blanchard hung up, cursing at the way his hand trembled. He unhooked the scrambler and put it back in his bag. He stood for a long time at the window, watching the snow accumulate on the sidewalks, imagining how it would be when the Veil was torn and the Garou were exposed.
    Not many believers at first, except perhaps those who saw the deed. Then the word would spread. Especially, he thought, if he could get television to record the proof.

His lips twitched.

There would be coverage tonight. The costume thing. Local news. Stringers, or reporters who were at the bottom of the ladder. Unless . . .

His lips twitched.

Unless he made a couple of calls, let a couple of people know that tonight wasn't just going to be a bunch of jerks walking around like it was Halloween.

Unless he let it slip that . . . that maybe the police were set to make a major arrest . . . that the killer was actually someone here at the convention.

Imagine, he thought.

Armageddon in Chattanooga.

It would almost be funny, if so many people weren't about to die.

Rich ebony fur edged in silver on crown and chest.

"Richard?"

"Yes."

Gently slanted eyes filled with green fire.

"Oh, God."

He said nothing.

"Oh, God, Richard, I think I'm gonna be sick."

23

He took his time dressing, all the while listening to Joanne in the bathroom, retching, moaning, stumbling around, retching and moaning again. Once, he heard a fist slam against the wall. He opened the drapes and turned off the lights. He watched the snow as it began to turn over to sleet. He knocked on the bathroom door and didn't react when she screamed at him to go away. She was terrified, and terrified that she might be going insane; she would find a hundred reasons why she hadn't seen what she had, and a hundred more why all of them wrong; she might huddle in there for hours, believing she was dreaming until she knew that she was awake; she would rehearse what she would tell the others, and she would weep and scream again.

Because she knew no one would believe her.

And there was nothing, not now, he could do to help her through it.

He couldn't stay. He had to trust his own judgment and hope that she would make the right decision.

On a pad of hotel stationery he left a short note, picked up his jacket, and left without a good-bye. On the way to the elevator he caught up with the white-haired man he had met on the first night, who smiled wanly in greeting. He looked exhausted, massively hung over, and Richard couldn't help a sympathetic smile.

"Rough night?" he asked as they stepped into the car.

A woman's voice called plaintively just as the doors closed.

"Insatiable," he groaned.

"Doesn't sound too bad to me."

Marcus Spiro chuckled. "At my age, it either kills you or makes you younger."

"And?"

The door opened on the gallery floor.

"Well, my hair is still white, but I'm not dead. Could be worse," and he left with a wave over his shoulder.

Richard felt himself grinning as he rode down to the first floor, and felt the grin fade as he stepped into the nearly empty lobby. Not all the chairs and sofas were taken; those people he did see were clearly on their way to someplace else. Despite the noise he heard from the gallery above, down here the world was hushed. After a moment's indecision, he made his way to an alcove that contained public telephones and tried to call John Chesney, but again there was no response; nor could he raise Viana or Maurice.

He almost dialed Fay's number.

Until he remembered.

Disturbed, and feeling flashes of anger at being deserted, he wandered aimlessly around the first floor, noting the sheet of ice forming on the streets, looking through the window of the gift shop at the day's headlines in the local paper.

Another murder.

That stopped him until he saw "copycat killer" in the body of the text. He went in and bought a copy, took it to the restaurant and ate a fast lunch while he read what little there was, plus a lengthy sidebar on the serial killer and his latest attack on the mountain. By the time he was finished, he suspected that the copycat killer wasn't a copycat at all.

It was someone who, for some reason, had tried to make things confusing.

No, he thought; not some reason.

Had Richard not been injured, he might well have gone to the bus station himself, just to be sure the rogue hadn't struck again. And if he had . . . a trap, John had warned him; this whole affair may well be a trap.

Feeling more alert, he wandered back to the lobby, noting what his preoccupation had prevented him from seeing the first time around—more than a dozen easels scattered around the room, each holding a large color photograph. From the legends at the bottom, not all of which he understood, the pictures appeared to be of stellar attractions of previous costume events at this annual convention, and he had to admit that many of them were quite amazing, detailed and elaborate, and, in some cases, astoundingly beautiful.

And some were rather silly.

He couldn't help a quick laugh when he stopped in front of a picture of someone who had chosen to be Lon Chaney, Jr.'s Wolf Man. A remarkably faithful rendition of the motion-picture monster, with the added attraction of a busty, scantily clad Gypsy cowering at his furry feet.

Oh brother, he thought, holding back a laugh; boy, if they only knew.

"Interesting," a voice said blandly beside him.

He looked as he said, "Excuse me?", then

shrugged an apology when he realized the man who had spoken had made the comment to his female companion. "Sorry."

"Not at all," the man answered with a polite smile. "We were admiring the picture gallery." He waved a hand at the other easels.

"So was I."

The woman, whose wiry hair had been pulled back into a fluffy ponytail, looked him over and looked away; her boredom couldn't have been more evident if she had worn a sign.

"It's amazing what these people can do," the man remarked, then cleared his throat. "I'm awfully sorry, I'm being rude." He held out his hand. "Blanchard. Miles Blanchard. This is my wife, Wanda."

Richard shook the hand without giving his own name, nodded to the woman, who hadn't looked back, and gestured toward the Wolf Man. "I gather these people are pretty heavily into movies and TV."

"Looks that way, yes. It must take them hours to put some of these costumes together, don't you think?"

Richard supposed that it would, spotted the badge on the man's chest, and asked if he too was going to be in costume that night.

"But of course," Blanchard answered with an expansive laugh. He slipped his arm around his wife and hugged her close; she didn't react. "We wouldn't think of not doing it. It's a tradition, you might say."

Richard heard someone call his name.

"Right . . . honey?"

"What will you be?" he asked as he looked around, and saw Joanne in the middle of the lobby, beckoning urgently. "Hey, I'm sorry," he said quickly, stepping away. "I have to go. Nice meeting you. Good luck."

Blanchard said something in response, but Richard didn't listen. Anxious and hopeful, he hurried over to

Joanne, who immediately grabbed his hand and dragged him toward the staircase leading to the gallery floor.

"Come on, there's something I have to show you."

He tugged on her arm, wanting to see what he could read in her eyes. "Are you. . . ?"

"Shut up," she said without much heat. "No, I'm not, but shut up."

They pushed through the crowd, Joanne taking him through the ballroom's wide anteroom to the gallery's other side, then up three steps into a long corridor where more photographs were on display. Some guests were already in costume, but Richard saw that these weren't anywhere near on par with those in the pictures. Mostly capes and fangs, or what resembled *Star Trek* uniforms, and one white-faced guy in a fuzzy black wig, net stockings, high heels, and a fancy black corset.

Richard couldn't help but stare as the man and his similarly dressed retinue passed, and Joanne had to yank his hand twice before she got his attention.

"Look," she ordered, and pointed.

"Jo," he said, "I've already seen a picture of the Wolf Man downstairs."

"Look, damn it."

He did, and the hall fell silent, nothing but a rush of dry wind in his ears.

It wasn't the Wolf Man.

It was a Garou.

According to the legend, the picture had been taken just two years ago.

He couldn't breathe.

Joanne pulled him away toward a narrow staircase in the opposite wall.

Garou. Here. And it's been here for at least two years.

"Come on," she said tightly.

He stopped halfway down, nearly pulling her off her feet.

"What?"

"Not a rogue," he said. "I'll be damned. It's not a rogue."

The restaurant/bar was packed, and too many people stood in line. Impatiently she pulled him back into the hall, frowned in thought for a moment, then said, "Button your coat, we're going out."

They went across the boulevard to a McDonald's on the other side. The light inside was too bright for the weather, the colors too vivid, the smells too strong. Every sound too sharp, every move too stilted.

Like being in the corner of a glaringly lit stage surrounded by the night.

He didn't want anything, but she nearly filled a tray, and they took a booth along a fake-brick wall. She fussed a bit with her food, setting it out as if she were having a real meal, then pointed at the fries.

"Am I going to be able to keep this stuff down?"

His smile was automatic and genuine. "I hope so."

"Good, 'cause I'm starving. And while I eat, you're going to tell me everything, okay? Everything I need to know."

"Why?"

"I'm your partner, right? If you're going to hunt this thing, I—"

He slammed a fist on the table, making her jump, eyes wide and fearful.

"Son of a bitch!"

"What? What's wrong? Did I say something wrong?"

He shook his head, put his hands to his head and

shook it angrily. "There was a man and woman in the lobby. I was talking to them when you—"

"I saw them. So what?"

"They belong to the convention. I asked if they were going to be in costume, and he said they were." He lowered his hands, palms down, to the table. "I didn't catch what he said right away, when I asked him what he'd be. I was too worried about what . . ." He stopped himself and looked around the restaurant, shook his head at his own stupidity, and forced the tension out of his system. "He said, 'Hunter,' Jo. He said, 'We'll be hunters, Mr. Turpin.'"

There was a delay in her comprehension, but when it came it knocked her back in her seat. "What?"

"He knew my name, Jo. He knows who I am."

"Don't bother," she said when he started to get up. "He did it deliberately, to get your attention. And he's not going to be there, waiting for you to come back." She picked up a hamburger, grimaced at it, and took a bite.

"You're eating."

"I told you, I'm starving." She took another bite. "Now talk to me, Richard. How does he know who you are?"

He explained briefly about the Warders, stumbling when he mentioned Fay, and those the Garou knew were trying to gather information about their world. It had been previously thought that these other groups, however many there were, were too disparate to cause many problems because, like humans generally, they hoarded knowledge for the sake of power, and for the sake of future glory. Bad for the humans, good for the Garou, because it made it easier for them to keep tabs on what these people knew, and what they thought they knew.

When they learned too much, group members tended to disappear.

Joanne stabbed a french fry into a thick puddle of catsup. "By disappear, you mean . . ."

"Yes."

There was no guilt, no remorse, he told her; it was a simple matter of survival, for the Garou and for Gaia. Humans didn't realize it, but it was for their survival too. But now someone had slipped through the Garou net.

"This guy Blanchard."

"No. He's working for someone else. People like this, they don't dirty their own hands."

She met his gaze without blinking. "Like the Warders."

He didn't deny it.

Nor could he deny any longer that one of the Warders may have ordered Fay's death, undoubtedly because he knew she had warned him, knew where her primary allegiance lay. And perhaps she knew more, something she hadn't been able to tell him.

"She was your lover."

He nodded.

"Children?" She gave him a lopsided grin. "Or whatever?"

He returned the grin, and shook his head. Garou who mated, no matter how much in love, rarely produced normal offspring. These métis, as they were called, were deformed if they lived, already mad, already half dead. He glanced away, suddenly uncomfortable. He damn near started blushing. "Garou like me come from . . . I guess—"

"A mixed marriage?" she suggested.

"Close enough." He still wouldn't look at her. "Wolves or humans, actually."

She nodded thoughtfully, and ate another fry.

"You know, some people would think that's pretty gross."

"And you?" he asked without thinking.

"Don't push it, Richard, I'm still working on it, okay?" When he held up his hands, she added, "But now we have to figure out a way to get you out of the city in one piece."

"No," he said. "First, I have to figure out how to take care of the false rogue. Then I take care of Blanchard and whoever's with him, probably that woman. Then I get out of town."

She gaped, started to argue, then slumped in defeat and said, "Well, maybe I can help you out."

"How?"

"I think I know who that rogue thing is."

24

They reached the exit just as a band of convention-eers scrambled in out of the sleet and rain. Their voices were too loud, their faces too animated, their apologies as they bumped into Joanne and Richard too filled with uncaring laughter.

Joanne hooked her arm around Richard's, and they went outside, unable to move quickly because the footing was too slippery. The wind had picked up, the sleet falling at an angle that stung his ear and cheeks. At the curb they were forced to wait for a bus that skidded and hissed steam as it stopped for a red light. Once on the island, they had to wait again, this time for a funeral, headlamps aglare, the mourners unseen in gleaming black limousines. Slush had already begun to form in the gutters; there was nothing left of the morning's snowfall but a few patches in recesses the sleet couldn't reach.

Once under the hotel's canopy, however, he pulled her to one side, put his arms around her back and clasped his hands behind her. She resisted for only a second, shivering, cheeks beginning to blotch with pale red.

"When I go in there, it begins," he said, nodding toward the double glass doors.

"We," she reminded him. "I still have to tell you."

"Me," he contradicted gently. "Lt. Millson will kill me if you don't show up for that meeting."

"Can he?" She cocked her head, smiling.

"No. Not really. But it's the thought that counts, Jo. You still have a job. It means too much to you, and I don't want you to lose it."

He could tell she knew he was right. He could also tell that she didn't want to let go. Not now. Not for a long time.

"What are you going to do?"

"Right now?" He frowned over her head, his breath drifting into her hair like pale smoke. "Not much. And certainly not in there. There are too many people, too many eyes, if you know what I mean." He shuddered when a run of ice water slipped from his hair down his neck and to his spine. "First thing I must do is make some calls. I have to know what's happened to my . . . to the Warders."

"Stay away from your room," she warned.

"Why?"

"They got you once, remember? If you stay alone, they'll try to get you again."

He wanted to tell her that he could take care of himself, but an image of the silver spike in his bathroom flared and vanished. He didn't think that this Miles Blanchard would be carrying a club. He'd have a gun. Silver bullets. He had a partner. More silver.

"Damn," he whispered.

The sleet had turned to mostly rain, and it fell heavily, springing fountains in the street, drumming hard on the canvas canopy, sounding like the thunder of a stampede.

"Okay." She poked his chest with a stiff finger.

"Use the public phones, stay out of crowded rooms—and empty ones—and keep yourself visible. All the time, Richard, all the time."

He slipped his arms away and gripped her shoulders. "I can't."

"Why?" she demanded.

"I have to go someplace first."

"What? Listen, Richard, you can't—"

He silenced her with a finger. "This is something I must do, and it's a place where you can't go. It won't take long by your time, but I have to do it if I'm going to have a chance."

Her protest sputtered on, but it was only words without meaning. She lay her palm against his chest. "This is some kind of . . . Garou thing?"

He nodded.

"Is it dangerous?"

"Not yet. I won't lie to you, Jo. It could be, but not yet."

"And when you get back?"

"I will do exactly what you told me. I swear it." He shook his head. "No. I give you my word."

She snapped a thumb toward the parking lot. "My car's over there. I'll be back as fast as I can." With a sly smile she patted her breast pocket. "I still have the key."

"Call the room first, look for me," he said sternly.

"Hey," she said, insulted. "I'm a cop, gimmie a break, okay?"

There was nothing left to say, and without bothering to think, he pulled her close again, and he kissed her, soft and quickly on the lips.

Flustered, she broke away and hurried to the curb, hurried back and said, "I have to get one thing straight, all right?"

"Sure."

"When you say this Garou thing, these people of

yours, we're talking about . . ." She swallowed and looked sheepish.

He couldn't help but grin. "Yes, Jo, I'm talking about werewolves."

She nodded sharply. "Good. Okay. Just wanted to be sure."

Seconds later the rain took her, smearing her to a formless figure that disappeared when she crossed the street. He waited a moment longer, then went inside and gasped at the too-warm air that hit him from a ceiling vent. He took off his jacket and shook it hard, away from his side, then grabbed it in the middle and headed for his room.

The desert was silent.

He made his way through the ruins to the garden, and sat in the chair where Fay's spirit had been.

The stone vase was still there.

The rose was gone.

He looked at the table, sighing when he saw the thin layer dust from the drying of her black tear. He passed a hand over it, and the dust scattered and was gone, and he wished, too late, he had kept some of it for himself.

Emerald sky and gold-tinged light.

No one came, nothing moved.

He rose and began to walk, skirting the barren flower beds, searching the crumbling stone paths for something, anything, that would send him where he needed to go.

The rogue wasn't a rogue.

He came to a low wall and fingered the brittle straw that poked out of the mud.

The photograph in the hallway.

He followed the wall around the garden's perimeter,

breaking off straw, crumbling bits of clay between his fingers.

Fay's warning.

He stopped at a tree, whose bark was sickly gray, whose branches were bent and twisted as if in frozen torment. There were no leaves. The knees of a root broke through the faded tiled floor.

It was inconceivable that a Garou could be so careless a hunter. The monthly pattern was deliberate, deliberately staged to attract the Warders' attention. To attract him. And it had worked. But to hunt a Garou who has lost touch with Gaia and his mind was one thing; to hunt one in control, to hunt one as he had hunted the rabbit, was something he wasn't sure he could do, no matter what tribe the false rogue belonged to. It fell too close to blasphemy. Too close to treason.

Emerald sky and black-emerald clouds.

Gold-tinged light.

The soughing of a slow wind sifting sand from the wall, the grains falling through the dead tree like the scratch of ice against glass.

This man called Blanchard. He knew Richard, knew him by name and most likely, therefore, knew who and what he was. Did he work with the Garou whose picture was in the hall? Or was there a third party, unknown to both?

Why the hell wouldn't the Warders return his calls?

He punched the trunk in frustration, and a thin branch swayed under the impact, snapped, fell, shattered to pieces at his feet.

And something moved on the bark.

It startled him into taking a step backward, then puzzled him into drawer nearer again.

He smiled, but briefly.

A chameleon, ridged skin almost the exact hue of

the bark, moved ponderously around the trunk
toward the thick stump of a branch. Its tail was
blunt, its sawtooth back broad, its head marked by a
pair of forward-aiming horns.

Gently Richard picked it up and carried it in his
palm to the table, sat, and watched it lumber toward
the vase.

Gray shifted to sandstone.

Almost, but not quite.

He leaned back and stretched out his legs, crossing them at the ankles, studying the little beast,
watching it try to vanish. One hand shook the table
slightly, and the chameleon froze, sandstone lids
slipping over its bulbous eyes.

Now. Now it was gone.

The soughing became a keening, and beneath it a
deep calling that turned his head toward the tree. In
the uppermost branches, the ones that formed
jagged cracks in the emerald-streaked sky, he saw a
bird, huge and brown.

"Ah," he said, and nodded to it. "I've been wondering where you've been."

The owl's wings spread, and the wind took it aloft.

He followed its effortless glide above the ruins,
shifted back a little when the owl began its glide,
wings high, talons out, soundless save for the wind,
until it swept with a rush across the table and vanished over the far, falling wall.

He had to brush a hand across the table to make
the chameleon was actually gone.

The keening became a roar.

He didn't keep track of the time he sat there.

Time, in the desert, meant less than nothing.

When he finally rose, he lifted his face to the wind
and the emerald sky and the hunter bird, and he
shifted.

And he bellowed until walls began to crack, and the stone vase exploded.

Shifted again and walked to the nearest gate.

When his shadow brushed the tree, the tree shimmered and fell to dust, twisting slowly in the wind.

He opened his eyes, feeling the desert heat still radiating from his skin. He sat cross-legged in the center of the bed, stripped to the waist, feet bare, hands cupped lightly over his knees.

In the middle of the sitting room, Joanne sat in a chair, legs out, hands in her jeans pockets.

"You were gone a long time," she said when he allowed himself a smile of greeting.

"I guess." His voice was hoarse, his throat dry. "It's hard to tell sometimes."

She glanced at the window. "The sun's down."

He eased himself to the edge of the mattress, grimacing as he straightened his legs. "Then it was a long time."

"Where . . . where were you?"

"Away. I'm sorry, but that's the best way I can describe it. Away. In a place, like I said, where I'd hoped to find some answers."

"Did you?" She hadn't moved.

He shivered a little in the room's cool air. "I don't know. I think so. It's hard to tell sometimes. Things where I was, they aren't always what they seem."

She moistened her lips. "And sometimes they are?"

"Yep."

"So how do you know the difference?"

He laughed quietly. "Practice. And a whole ton of mistakes."

She drew her feet back toward the chair and sat up. "You made a noise there, at the end."

He raised an eyebrow. "I did?"

"Kind of a grunting or something. Like you were growling."

He looked at her in admiration. "You know, Detective, you're taking all this damn calmly."

"The hell I am." She wiped a hand under her nose. "I'm sitting in a room with a half-naked man, who, if you can believe it, can turn himself into a wolf."

"A sort of wolf."

"Whatever. And he tells me there are others like him, all over the damn place. One of them, he tells me, is the guy I'm after. Then he sits there, on that bed, in some kind of spooky trance, doesn't move a muscle for hours, makes me think maybe he's some kind of dead, makes these noises that scares the shit out of me, then has the nerve to tell me that I'm taking all this damn calmly."

She took a deep breath.

"You could have been killed, you stupid son of a bitch." Her voice deepened. "Anyone could have come in here while you were like that, and you could have been killed!"

"I would have known, Jo. I would have sensed it."

"You could have been killed," she insisted, and something glittered in her eyes. Then she spat dryly. "Calmly. Good . . . Lord."

Another deep breath.

"And if you don't stop looking at me like that, Turpin, I'm going to scream my frigging head off."

He laughed. He couldn't help it, it just started, and once started, he couldn't stop it. When she stood, fists at her side, he raised his hands in apology, laughed even harder, and fell onto his back, bounced to a sitting position, and she was there, right there, standing at his knees.

Hands still raised, he gulped for air, forced himself

to calm down, and hiccuped so loudly he started laughing again.

She stared.

"Oh, God." He shook his head violently. "Oh, God," and used the backs of his hands to wipe the tears from his eyes.

"The noise," she said evenly.

He looked into her eyes, and sobered. "Yes?"

"What did it mean?"

"I'm a hunter," he told her.

"I know that."

"It means the hunt has begun."

25

For a moment, just a moment, the lobby was empty.

Silent except for the distant sound of the wind.

A long table had been set up against the west wall, opposite the elevators, a white cloth draped over it, four chairs behind. The Green Room Restaurant's tall double doors were open, the tables inside the elegant dining room pushed against the walls. The easels had been taken down, the photographs gone.

For a moment, just a moment, nothing moved.

A cough, then, and a murmur as a group of people came out of the bar's rear entrance, their footsteps echoing until they reached the carpet.

The contest judges took their seats behind the table—an artist, a professional costumer designer, and an editor from the sponsoring publisher. The fourth chair was for the guest of honor, but Marcus Spiro hadn't yet arrived; no one seemed too concerned. Low voices from above as regular guests lined the gallery railings, while others drifted around the lobby perimeter. Waiting.

The muffled cry of a siren.

The sound of the wind.

When the elevator doors next opened, the evening began.

They drifted out in singles and in pairs, their costumes simple in the beginning—generations of *Star Trek*, uniforms and masks, and a few who had almost learned the art of latex and paint. *Star Wars*. *The Highlander*. A few capes and white faces and red-tipped fangs. *Doctor Who*. They were nervous despite their smiles, avoiding the judges' gazes, avoiding those who watched from above and behind. Walking slowly. Posing. Trying a bit too hard not to stare at the competition.

The doors opened.

The doors closed.

A princess from someone's book, in glitter and gown, with a page for an escort and a tiny dragon on her shoulder that spat sparks for fire; a Southern belle in a hoop skirt with a parasol and a wide-brimmed hat, with an exquisite leopard's face and a leopard's tail, and where flesh should have been there was fur; a satyr complete with cloven hooves and pointed ears; an impossibly tall Frankenstein's monster; a couple in Elizabethan dress, the woman carrying her grinning head under her arm, the man carrying an executioner's ax.

A slender figure dressed in shimmering black; when he raised his arms before the judges, his cloak was lined with black feathers edged in silver and gold.

Toad and Mole; Pinhead and the Candyman; Xena and Hercules; the Hunchback of Notre Dame and a scantily clad Esmeralda.

The lobby filled.

There was, here and there, a smattering of applause. A few catcalls and some laughter. Whistles. More applause.

Antennae and claws, rhinestones and feathers, chain mail and leggings.

They flowed smoothly in and out of the lobby and Green Room, the best always in character, whether fairy tale or nightmare.

The judges conferred and made notes, and the fourth chair remained empty.

Wanda leaned back against the wall beside the bar's entrance. To her right, some thirty yards away, was the hotel's Broad Street entrance; directly ahead was the boutique promenade that led to the parking garage entrance; and to her left another sixty feet distant were the backs of scores of people watching the costume contest.

Her hands were deep in her trench coat pockets, and though her expression was studiously blank, she was more than a little disturbed.

The storm had changed everything.

She could see the glitter of sleet turned to snow, and knew it was going to be hell getting out of the city tonight. She was a Georgia woman herself; she knew how folks down here reacted to unexpected winter storms like this, storms more suitable to places north of the Mason-Dixon line. If she wanted to put some distance between her and what pursuit there might be, she had to act within the hour, or she'd be lost.

In more ways than one.

Applause filled the lobby.

Beyond the heads of the onlookers, she spotted the glare of television lights.

Maybe she just ought to leave. Now. Crimmins could hardly blame her. A touch of sugar in her voice would smooth that old man's temper. Besides, there would be other times, other places, where her particular skills would be needed.

She didn't move.

Her left hand left its pocket and touched the back of her head, touched the lump Blanchard had left there.

A spattering of laughter; a few more catcalls and whistles.

The crowd shifted, people exchanging places, coming down the stairs from the gallery, going up in search of a better view.

The hand returned to her pocket.

Her priorities had changed. Turpin was no longer at the head of the list. He would die if she had the opportunity, but she wanted Miles Blanchard.

Not dead; that would be too easy.

What she would do, what her silver blade would do, would make sure that nothing in that stupid kit of his would ever be able hide him again.

He would be, quite literally, a marked man.

And only then, when she felt like it, would she cut out his heart and shove it down his throat.

The elevator doors opened, and Beauty and the Beast stepped out, courtly and splendid.

One more time, Richard thought, dropping wearily onto the couch and grabbing the telephone; one more time.

Jo stood in front of him, hands on her hips. "You're stalling."

Chesney didn't answer his phone; neither did Viana or Poulard.

He could hear the patter of sleet on the pane behind him, punched by the wind.

"Richard, come on, you're stalling."

With a disgusted noise he replaced the receiver and looked out at the city. The lights were extra bright, and a car skidded across the intersection in maddeningly slow motion.

Her voice was quiet and hard: "They say, you have an idea, Detective? You think you have a hunch? Fine. Pursue it on your own time, don't come crying to us when you get burned, 'cause we don't know you."

He shifted his gaze to her face.

"If you're right, they take the credit; if you're wrong, they've already put the distance between you, and you get all the blame when the shit comes down."

He shook his head. "It's not the same, Jo."

"They've cut you loose, Richard, and you know it. Think about what they said to you, for God's sake. They never really expected you to bring this rogue thing back alive, and you know it. But because you're you, they expect you to try, and they don't expect you to come back at all."

"No. It's not like that."

"Oh, yeah, it is," she contradicted softly, reached out and grabbed his hand. Pulled gently until he stood. "Yeah, Richard, it is."

"If you're so smart, you want to tell me why?"

She grinned. "I'm working on it."

So am I, he thought reluctantly; so am I.

"Meanwhile, we get this rogue who isn't really a rogue, right?" She slipped on her jacket, clipped her holster onto her belt at the small of her back.

"And I suppose you know who it is."

She stared at him, surprised. "Well, sure. Leon Hendean."

He gaped.

She reminded him of their talk with Curly Guestin,

that he had complained that he hadn't been the one to fix the glider Trish McCormick had used the day she'd died. No one else worked at the place, except its owner. No one else had been there the day of the murder, except Hendean. If, she continued as they left the room, Richard could go down the mountain-side, so could Hendean; it was entirely possible he had planned the woman's death. Maybe Curly had figured it out, and had to be killed for it. As well, she added, as to bring more attention to himself.

"To get me down here."

She nodded.

He rubbed the back of his neck absently, follow-ing her down the hall. "No proof, though."

"We'll get it. Be patient. First, we have to get hold of our boy."

They passed the elevator alcove, and she pointed toward an open door, down on the left. "In there. The brain center of the convention."

"How do you know?"

"I'm a detective, Turpin, remember? I detect."

She motioned to him to say nothing when they reached the room, and he leaned against the jamb, hands in his pockets, trying to look as official as he could.

It was a similar set-up to his, except the bedroom was to the left. On the couch opposite the door sat a middle-aged stocky man with black hair in an incon-gruous Caesar cut. White shirt. Trousers. The table in front of him littered with pizza boxes and clipboards. A blank look on his rounded face when Joanne stepped in, held up her ID, and said, "Chattanooga police. You in charge here?"

He nodded mutely.

"You got a name?"

"Attco," he said, and pushed himself hurriedly to

his feet. "Holburton Attco." He shrugged sheepishly. "What can I say? My mother's a nut. They call me Holly."

"Well, Holly," Joanne said, "I need you to answer a few questions, all right?"

He blinked. His face paled, then reddened, and he glared at the ceiling. "Godammit! Underage drinkers, right? Some asshole made a complaint, right?" He stomped around the coffee table and took a swipe at a blank computer terminal. "No. It's some asshole walking around with a sword out or something, right? Jesus!" He looked at Richard for the first time and spread his arms. "I got a zillion people working security around here, you know? But they can't be everywhere. I mean, Jesus, why the hell would anyone call the police, for Christ's sake? It's not like we're tearing the place apart." He stomped back to the couch and dropped onto it. "God." He glanced at his watch. "Aw, Jesus, the masquerade's begun and I'm not down there. I'm supposed to be down there, you know." He snapped his fingers. "Shit, one of them's naked, right? Oh God, please tell me one of them isn't naked."

Joanne sniffed, and rubbed the side of her nose. "You finished?"

"I . . . yeah. I guess."

"Leon Hendean. You know him?"

Attco frowned his puzzlement. "Well, sure. He's part of the committee." Another frown, this time thinking. "He's a liaison this year."

Joanne waggled a hand in silent question.

"He works with the guests," the man explained. "Runs errands for them, keeps them happy, gets them where they're supposed to be . . . on time, with any luck."

"And where would he be now?"

Attco shrugged. "How the hell should I know? With Spiro, I suppose."

"Spiro?"

"The main speaker," Richard said. When Joanne looked at him, he nodded down the hall. "I've run into him a couple of times. That's his room, by—" He caught himself, jerked a thumb. "The one with the double doors."

"Right," said Attco. "You find him, you'll find Leon. But why?"

"Those pictures in the lobby, Mr. Attco," she said with a polite smile.

"The pictures?" Attco scratched his paunch, confused by her change of subject. "Oh. Yeah. Costume winners from past years. We put them up this year because a couple of the publishers put up some serious bucks for the winner this time. Incentive, see?"

"How serious?" Richard asked.

"Fifteen hundred for the Best in the Show. A couple of five hundreds for the others."

"Not bad."

"Hey," he said. "It's not my money, and it brought in the experts."

"And their money."

Attco grinned. "That, too."

"The one of the werewolf," Joanne said, giving Richard a look to keep him quiet. "Has a Gypsy at his feet?"

Attco nodded eagerly. "Oh, man, yeah. That was two years ago, I think. Most amazing thing I ever saw." His hands shaped the air in front of him. "You couldn't see anything, man, it was incredible. No seams, no Velcro, no zippers, no nothing. Had the most unbelievable contact lenses. Big. I mean, huge guy. The woman was someone he'd picked up for the

weekend. She had to lead him around, I don't think
he could see hardly anything with all that makeup."
His enthusiasm faded for a moment, his expression
abruptly somber. "No competition that time, believe
it. He walked off with everything."

"You said 'was,'" Richard said, ignoring Joanne's
warning glance. "About the lady."

"Yeah." Attco fussed with some papers on the
table. "She died two weeks later. Committed suicide."

"How?"

The man looked at him almost angrily. "Fucking
jumped off Lookout Mountain, that's how. There
wasn't much left of her when they found her, okay?"

Richard backed off, hands up in apology.

"Hendean," Joanne said into the silence.

Attco blinked. "What?"

"The werewolf guy. There was no name on the picture, like on the others. But it was Hendean, right?"

"Leon?"

Joanne nodded.

"Leon?" He rubbed his forehead. "Son of a bitch,
you know, you might be right?" He laughed. "Son of
a bitch."

The elevator doors opened, and Death stepped out,
his scythe tipped in red.

Blanchard tossed the last of his gear into the rental
car, cursing the weather, and cursing himself for
playing the role of the gentleman assassin. Taking
his time. Revealing himself to his victim. Toying.
Playing. Making it a game.

Vanity, it was. Foolish, foolhardy vanity that might

actually have worked if the weather had given him time to play the game. Now he had to hurry. Now he had to believe his decision was the right one.

He had already made one sweep around the lobby, had seen the elaborate outfits, the cameras, the audience, and realized that Crimmins' order to rend the Veil was a joke. Any Garou could walk in there now and not be noticed; any death would be seen as part of the show, an act, a skit, and no one would care.

Crimmins, for the first time in their long association, was wrong.

And he had been wrong for thinking it would work.

For the fifth or sixth or dozenth time he made sure he had his passports, the bank books, all the identification all his personalities needed to leave the country a millionaire several times over. Then he checked the chamber of his gun, smiling at the silver, slipped it into his topcoat pocket, and headed for the hotel.

The hell with the Garou.

Richard Turpin was the prey.

The elevator doors opened.

A werewolf stepped out.

26

Richard paced the empty hall outside Attco's room. Prowling. Nervous. He could feel the storm surround the hotel; he could feel the energy out there, and in here; he could feel a subtle shift in the balance of the way things were, a shift that meant the hunt.

As he paused at the door, puzzling over a whiff of something familiar, he was distracted when he heard Joanne demand, "What do you mean, might be? Don't you know?"

Attco shrugged. "Nope."

"How the hell could you not know? You're supposed to be in charge, right?"

"Yeah, but you haven't any idea what these—" The telephone rang, and Attco stumbled around the coffee table to grab the receiver. "Yeah?"

Richard couldn't catch all that was said; he was too busy watching the anger and disappointment on Joanne's face.

"Hey." Attco slammed the receiver back onto its cradle. "Gotta go, sorry. They need me downstairs. Some TV people have shown up."

Joanne grabbed his arm as he headed out. "So who would know?"

"Know what?"

"Who the werewolf was?"

"Jesus, lady, I don't know. Look, meet me downstairs after I take care of the TV thing, I'll show you who's in charge this year, okay? Come on, I gotta go."

Richard stepped aside as Attco hurried down the hall, but shook his head when Joanne beckoned him to join her.

"What?" Her eyes narrowed in suspicion.

"Just go. I'll catch up."

She started to argue, then scowled and ran when Attco called out that he had an elevator waiting.

When she was gone, he went straight to the stairwell and let himself out on the gallery floor. As quickly as he could, he pushed through the crowd, excusing himself, smiling, nodding, making his way around to the other side where luck gave him a place beside one of the pillars. From here he could see the elevator doors, and nearly laughed aloud when the werewolf made its entrance.

Just like one of the pictures he had noted earlier: Lon Chaney, Jr., right out of any one of a half-dozen Universal pictures. Hairy face and black clothes, hairy feet and hands. It wasn't bad, but it wasn't real.

A few seconds later, the other door opened, and he watched Joanne follow Attco through the audience and contestants, Joanne tugging angrily at the man's arm, the man glaring at her while, at the same time, trying to smile at a man with a microphone standing beside another man with a TV camera on his shoulder.

Richard searched the lobby intently, watching as the contestants seemed to be forming a line out of the chaos, a line that wound past a table

below him and into, and out of, the Green Room
to his left. Behind him, he heard someone complaining about the guest of honor not showing up
for the judging, heard someone else laugh and say
he was probably hiding in the bar, looking to get
laid.

Another sweep of the costumes, and he wasn't
sure if he was relieved or disappointed.

No Garou. No one who matched Hendean's
description.

He eased back from the railing, his place instantly
taken by two giggling youngsters in capes, and made
his way back the way he had come, struggling not to
snarl when elbows stabbed his ribs and back, when
boots trod on his feet.

The noise level rose.

The lights dimmed, and were made dimmer by
vivid spotlights fixed to the pillars that skated slow-
moving circles across the lobby floor.

The glare caused everything else to fall into false
shadow.

On the gallery the crowd grew more raucous in the
near twilight, and twice Richard had to push people
out of his way. No longer polite. Frustration had weak-
ened the hold on his temper. What he wanted was to
get away from all these bodies, the smell of their
sweat, the smell of beer and liquor and cheap makeup
and damp clothes; what he wanted to shift and send
them all screaming to the comfort of their nightmares.

A burly man in a T-shirt grabbed his arm. "Hey,
mac, watch it, okay?"

Richard glared up at him. "What?"

The man nodded to a woman beside him, sucking
on the heel of her hand. "Made her cut herself, you
asshole."

Richard froze.

"You gonna apologize or what?"

He looked at the man without blinking.

. . . *green* . . .

"Hey."

. . . *fire* . . .

The hand gripping his arm fell away, and Richard
shoved his way clear, sprinted to the fire stairs and
took them up, two at a time. He slammed through
the door and swung around the corner, stopped at
his room and waited.

There it was.

The scent he had noticed earlier.

Slowly he approached the double doors of the
suite at the end of the short hall.

In there.

It was in there.

He tried the knob, but the door was locked, and
the lock was too strong for him to force.

It was in there.

The blood.

Joanne gave up.

Attco wasn't about to talk to her, not when he was
too busy sucking up to the newsman and the camera.

She supposed she could have reminded him who
she was, but that would attract the newsman's attention, and she didn't think the lieutenant would
appreciate it, not when she wouldn't be able to give
him a good reason why she was still here.

She let the crowd ease her away, forcing her
slowly toward the back. What she would do is find
Richard, find out why he had left her, and then—

A hand cupped her shoulder, and something hard
pressed into her back.

She didn't move.

A voice in her left ear: "Officer," it said, "you take one breath without my permission, and you won't breathe again."

Richard *shifted*.

Merged.

He pressed his hands against the wood, testing its strength, feeling its weakness, then took a step back and threw himself at the door.

It shuddered.

He did it again.

It bowed.

He snarled and did it a third time.

The crack of splintering wood was quick and sharp, like a gunshot.

The fourth time, the doors flew inward, and he leapt inside, great head swiveling as he tracked the scent of the blood.

A single lamp was lit by the bed.

He smelled the body first, then saw it curled in the shadows on the far side of the mattress.

Or what was left of it.

With the hand guiding her, and refusing to permit her to look around, she stepped slowly backward.

"Where is Turpin?"

She shook her head—I *don't know*.

The pressure on her back increased sharply.

"Where is he?"

She shook her head again, wondering why the hell nobody could see what was happening.

"One more time, cop." The pressure on her back increased sharply. "Where the fuck is he?"

There was a singular explosion of cheers and applause, and without thinking she stopped, and looked through a momentary gap in the crowd.

"Oh my God," she said.

And the voice answered, "You lose.

He stood in the ruined doorway, trembling with rage, green fire eyes dark enough to be black.

He hesitated only long enough to glance behind him once more, then raced down the hall.

Without changing.

Punching the metal fire door open, leaving a dent in its pocked surface, swinging over the railing and landing lightly on the floor below, again to reach the ground floor, grabbing the bar and shoving, shoving the door open and striding out, shifting into the open, into the shadowy dim light.

He heard the applause and the cheers, saw to his right a score or more people pushing forward to get a closer look at whatever enthralled them.

He saw Joanne.

In the spotlight, its deep gray fur glittered as though it had been touched by dew, its eyes glowed crimson, its teeth not quite white.

The Garou acknowledged the adulation with upraised arms and, in the silence that ensued, it lifted its muzzle and howled.

The hand turned Joanne around.

"Amazing, isn't it?" said Miles Blanchard. "A monster like that in clear view, and no one even knows."

She didn't look down; she knew the gun was in his pocket, too close to miss. Nor did she bother to tell him that shooting her now would be a huge mistake. Witnesses. A TV camera. None of it mattered, because they were all fixed on the creature in the spotlight. They may hear the shot, but Blanchard would be gone before anything could be done.

His smile was empty, his voice hollow and quiet. "No time for games, Detective. Tell me where he is and walk away, no catch, no tricks." The smile died. You have no idea, my dear. No idea at all."

She could feel her own weapon pressed against her spine, but they were two steps away from the crowd now, and he would spot any move.

There were giggles, then, and outright laughter. Speculation that the werewolf couldn't stand on his feet, that he was probably drunk.

"Turpin." Blanchard grabbed her shoulder again, and squeezed.

Use your knee, she told herself; just use your damn knee and get out of the way.

Instead, she said, "Look."

He didn't want to; she could see it, and she had to swallow a giggle when he glared an order at her.

And looked over his shoulder.

The Garou howled again.

There were cheers.

All the main lights were doused, nothing left but the spotlights in the lobby.

There were feigned screams of alarm, and nervous laughter.

Wanda didn't move.

She kept her hands in her pockets and thanked all the gods she knew that she'd been given this front-row seat.

With just a bit more luck, all her work would be done for her.

Nonetheless, she pressed a button on the ivory shaft, and a silver blade snicked out.

Just in case, she told herself.

Just in case.

Blanchard moved carefully, putting Joanne between him and Richard, shifting them all until they stood beside the gift shop's glass wall.

The applause was frantic now, the cheers boisterous.

"The thing is," Blanchard said mildly, his voice barely heard over the noise, "if you make a move, no matter what it is, the cop will die. Are you going to sacrifice her just to get at me, Turpin?"

"Standoff," Richard answered, just as evenly.

"No. I don't think so. What I think is, we'll move a little way down here, if you don't mind. Around the corner back there, by the bar door."

Then they'll separate, Richard thought; he'll keep us far enough away from him so that one shot will be all he needs.

He had no doubt what kind of bullets the gun had.

He had no doubt who would be first.

"And if you don't move, I'll kill her anyway," Blanchard added.

"Then you'll die."

"But she'll be dead."

He couldn't see her face, but he could feel her trembling, not all of it from fear. His left hand gently brushed across her shoulders, her back, fingers brushing over the bulge of her holster.

Blanchard looked and sounded calm, but he knew

it was as much a mask as those the contestants wore. It was more than simple fear; it was a sense of urgency. That might cause him to make a mistake, but it was just as likely to prompt him into acting without thinking. Whatever timetable he had, if Richard tried to stall, the trigger would be pulled anyway.

"Shall we?" Blanchard gestured with his chin. "Now, please?"

Richard didn't insult the man by faking resignation, but when he turned, taking Joanne's arm, he took only a few paces before he saw the woman leaning against the wall, one hand in her trench-coat pocket, the other tucked against her side.

"Your partner?" he asked over his shoulder.

"We have the same employer. That's all."

It made Richard stop.

"Damn it, Turpin."

At the same time, Joanne looked up at him, questioning without saying anything.

Blanchard prodded him with a sharp finger. "Move, damn it."

Richard remained where he was. "Jo, I was wrong."

The applause and cheers began to trail off behind them.

"Your friends," was all she said.

"Yeah. I was wrong. They're not involved at all."

Blanchard shoved him; he didn't move.

The woman straightened, keeping her hand at her side.

"I swear to Christ," Blanchard said tightly, "I'll do it right here, right now."

Richard faced him, and Blanchard took an involuntary step back.

"You work for the men who would destroy the Veil, don't you." He didn't expect an answer; he didn't need one. "Fay found out about you, didn't she." She hadn't been warning him about one of the Warders; she had been trying to warn him about this man, here.

Blanchard managed a sneer, but Richard knew it was only a cloak for his fear.

"Did you kill her?" Richard asked. His chest was tight, his breathing slow and deep. Specks of light coasted at the corners of his vision. "Did you?"

Blanchard blinked his confusion. "Who?" Then he shook himself, and pushed his gunhand against the topcoat fabric. "You're out of time, Turpin."

The lobby went silent.

Richard released Joanne's arm, leaned over and kissed her cheek. As he did, he whispered, "I'm sorry."

She kissed him back. "I'm not."

Blanchard's gun was free.

Richard heard the hammer cock as he turned back again.

He heard a collective gasp from the crowd, heard the Garou begin to snarl.

"Goddamn freak," Blanchard said, the gun aimed at Richard's heart. Richard had no choice. He used the only weapon he had. He lost his temper. And he shifted.

27

Light and shadows.

. . . green fire . . .

Richard's right hand shoved Joanne out of the way. Too hard. She stumbled, then fell as she tried to scramble her weapon from its holster.

Richard's left hand snared Blanchard's wrist, wrenching it up and away just as the gun fired.

Blanchard screamed.

Richard snarled.

Blanchard tried to backpedal, but Richard grabbed him between the legs and around the throat, and lifted him over his head, hearing nothing but the bloodlust storming in his ears, feeling the man squirming frantically in his grasp, inhaling the scent of the man's fear as if it were ambrosia.

He turned sharply, growling, and threw him down the hall, arms and legs flailing, skidding on his shoulder toward the exit, and the snow beyond.

He loped after him in the near dark, seeing nothing else but the man trying to get to his hands and knees, left arm useless, head hanging. He didn't care now if the contest spectators saw him, didn't care what they would say. He stood over Blanchard and waited.

Just waited.

Counting the seconds as the man finally tipped back on his heels and looked up and over his shoulder.

"No," Blanchard whispered. "Fucking freak, no."

"Turpin," he answered, voice guttural and harsh. "Remember me. I'm Richard Turpin."

His right arm lifted, claws flared, and swung down in an arc that seemed to move too slowly.

Blanchard couldn't move.

A flash, and the flesh of his face and throat grew thin dark lines; a flash, and the lines began to release smears of red; a flash, and his eyes were filled with swimming color; a flash, and he toppled forward, landing on his forehead. Kneeling as if in prayer.

Richard stared, not sated but satisfied.

A step back, a partial turn, and sudden fire stripped along his side.

He whirled, right leg buckling, and faced the woman, who smiled up at him over the tip of her silver blade.

"That was my party, you bastard," she said, nodding toward Blanchard's body.

He barely heard her.

The fire had taken root, and he could feel his own blood slipping through the ragged gash in his pelt. Beyond them, beyond the thunder of his pain, there was pandemonium. Screams and running feet and a high, hysterical howling.

Distracted, he missed the tension in Wanda's legs as she set herself to lunge.

And when she did, he realized he wouldn't be able to deflect the blade from taking root in his chest.

He didn't have to.

It was only a single gunshot, but it was enough.

Wanda gasped and arched her back, and a black-red rose blossomed on the front of her coat. She looked confused, then disappointed, before she fell against the wall and slid in stages to the floor.

"He's gone!" Joanne shouted at him, pointing with her gun toward the lobby. "He's out!"

They looked at each other for only a moment before he clamped an arm against his side and stumbled through the exit, into the storm and the quiet city.

The cold revived him somewhat as he swung around the corner of the building. It was difficult, but not impossible, to heal as he ran; he only hoped it would be enough when he came across the other Garou.

And this time he would.

Whatever this strange Garou's true intentions had been, they had resulted in Fay's death, and the near-killing of Joanne Minster. They had threatened everything he had sworn himself to protect.

Rogue or not, this Garou wouldn't last the night.

At the next corner he stepped into a howling wind, the snow blowing horizontally, directly into his eyes. But he saw a fleeing shadow far ahead, heading north toward the river, and he followed. Not racing. Using the time to let his body try to stitch the silver wound.

He slipped on ice.

The wind slammed him backward.

Snow clung to his fur in tiny balls of ice.

The street was dark, and made darker by the lonely islands of white cast by the streetlamps. At least the storm kept people inside, and as he shivered against the biting cold, he supposed he ought to be grateful for that.

He ran on.

Crosswinds at the intersections gave him excuses to pause, to catch his breath and check the healing—slow, too damn slow.

The Garou ahead could have plunged into any one of the side streets, but he didn't. He stayed just far enough ahead to keep himself indistinct, but not so far that Richard couldn't see him through the whirling flakes.

The cold.

Always the cold.

Always the mocking voice of the wind.

Across the street now, the bus station huddled in the dark, parking lot streaked with white and gray.

The Garou turned the next corner.

Richard followed, now just thirty yards behind, trying not to breathe ice into his lungs, concentrating on his footing and on the fire that finally began to dampen in his side.

The aquarium was just ahead.

The Garou darted across the road and ran beneath the entrance arch, turning abruptly as if he had suddenly forgotten his destination. He slid, waved one arm, and went down on both knees, sliding again until he slammed into the back of one of the benches, the impact stunning him and knocking him over onto his side.

Richard smiled.

There was no humor.

By the time the Garou had climbed to his feet, Richard was there.

Waiting.

The Garou braced himself against the bench, panting heavily, head almost bowed.

He's old, Richard thought in amazement; damn, he's old.

Here in the open, the storm pummeled them, stealing part of their attention, just enough to keep them both reasonably steady on their feet.

The snow matted in the Garou's fur added to Richard's belief.

"You're Spiro," he said, letting the wind spin his words.

Marcus Spiro lifted a weary arm in greeting.

"Why?"

Spiro's eyes, crimson fire, narrowed. "You think I'm a rogue?"

Richard shook his head. "No. But why?"

The Garou laughed, fangs not as long, not as sharp. "I was bored, you stupid boy. I was bored."

And before Richard could even begun to understand, Spiro sprang, claws at the ready, jaws snapping for Richard's throat.

For a second Richard couldn't fight, but the first stab of claw against the wound in his side changed that, and they grappled, snarling, snapping mostly at air, wrestling across the icy paving stones until the corner of the bench caught the Garou's hip, and he slipped.

Just enough.

Richard slammed an elbow into his temple, bringing him to his knees.

"No need," he said. "Come on, Spiro, there's no need anymore."

With surprising strength, Spiro launched himself from the ground, fangs scraping across the base of Richard's throat, burying a claw into the meat of his shoulder. The pain reignited the bloodlust, and Richard instinctively wrapped his arms around him, eventually spinning them both clumsily across the park while his teeth fought through the thick pelt to lay open the Garou's back.

A large shrub took them, and they fell, rolling down the slope.

Spiro opened a gash on Richard's chest.

Richard shoved him away and staggered to his feet, half blinded by the snow, deafened by the wind, arms hang loose at his side.

When Spiro charged again, howling his rage, the Strider caught him in the stomach with the claws of his right hand, pulled and turned, and let his jaws close around the back of Spiro's neck.

It didn't take very long.

He tasted the blood, felt the vertebrae snap, and shook his head violently, just to be sure.

Spiro didn't drop until Richard removed his claws.

And opened his jaws.

The twisted body slid toward the black water river.

Shifting.

Bleeding.

But Richard simply watched until the water took him away. Only then did he let his legs collapse; only then did he fall, onto his back to watch the snow spin in circles into his eyes.

28

The desert warmth soothed him, and made him shiver as he remembered the storm's needle cold.

The table was empty.

The chameleon tree was gone.

He didn't mind.

It was his place again, the place of sweet retreat.

Still . . . there was the voice.

He smiled, and stood, and walked among the ruins until he found a gate, took a breath, and stepped through.

"This is getting to be a habit, Turpin," Joanne said. She sat on the bed beside him, his shirt in her hands. "You do this often?"

There was still a faint burning in his side from Strand's silver blade, but the rest of his wounds had healed. No scars. Except inside.

She told him the hotel had been overrun by police shortly after Blanchard had died. When she told Lt. Millson the killer had been there—Blanchard's body the proof—and that it had most likely been Wanda

Strand—knife in hand, plus other assassin's weapons
found in her car—it had been fairly easy to convince
him that with the lights gone and all the shooting, it
wasn't hard to understand that a few hundred hyster-
ics thought a monster was on the loose.

A werewolf, if you can believe it.

A goddamn werewolf in Chattanooga.

"You're amazing," he said truthfully. "Absolutely
amazing."

She straightened, and grinned. "Damn right. He
bought every word." A hand brushed down his arm.
"I can see why those two wanted you dead. That
much I get. But I don't get Spiro. What did he mean,
he was bored?"

Richard still wasn't sure he understood it himself.
He had thought about it the entire time he had
dragged himself back to the hotel and managed,
with more than simple luck, to get back to his room.
He had thought about in his desert place. And he
thought about it now.

"He was old."

"So?"

"So when a Garou gets to a certain age, and it's
never the same for us all, we decide how we're going
to spend our last days. Human, or wolf. Whatever
will make the last times easier." He stared into the
sitting room; there were no lights but the glow from
outside. "I think . . . I guess he must have been a
fighter when he was young. I don't know. I do know,
from what he said to me the few times we talked,
that he wasn't entirely happy. That he was just going
through the motions."

"Until he died."

He nodded. "Yeah. I think so."

"So . . . what? He wanted to go out in a blaze of
glory or something?"

Richard thought a moment before smiling. "You know, you may be right. He was never a major writer. Never made the millions or had the fame other writers have." A shrug. "Maybe this was his way."

Joanne scratched a hand back through her hair. "Well, at least the Veil is okay, right?"

"Right." He hugged her with one arm. "You did fine, Detective. You did real fine."

She preened, she kissed him lightly, she slid off the bed before he could grab her and announced that she was starving. "I have reports, you know. But I'm not going to do them on an empty stomach. You owe me a meal." She started for the door, stopped, and turned around. "Cooked, Turpin. Cooked."

He dressed slowly, favoring the stiffness in his side, saying nothing when she told him she had taken a call from a man named John Chesney, who wanted to know if he was all right.

"I told him you were busy," she said. "I don't think he liked that."

Richard didn't care.

Changes were going to be made, and they were going to be made soon. He didn't appreciate how the Warders had apparently deserted him this time; he wanted answers, and he wouldn't leave them alone until he got them. Neither was he going to take another assignment until he himself was positive a rogue was on the loose.

What, he wondered, if there were others out there? Others like Marcus Spiro, who weren't content to take the usual path to dying? What if Gaia, whatever Her reasons, had caused an alteration in the way the Garou were supposed to protect her?

Changes.

There *would* be changes.

And there would be some answers.

"Are you away again?" Joanne demanded.

"No. Not really."

He joined her at the door, and she slipped an arm around his waist.

"Are you leaving town?"

"Soon. It's my job, remember?"

"How soon?"

Gently he pulled her arm from his waist and took her hand as he opened the door. "Not that soon, I don't think."

She grinned. "Good answer, Turpin."

At the elevators, she said, "Will you come back?"

"It might take time. But yes, I'll come back."

"Another good answer."

The doors opened; the car was empty.

She stepped in quickly, leaving him in the alcove. Joanne stood at the back of the elevator, lay a finger against her cheek, and said, "You ever make it with a cop?"

Richard felt his mouth open.

The doors began to close, and she made no move to stop them. "Wrong answer," she said with a slow shake of her head. And the doors shut as she added, "Take the stairs, it'll clear your mind."

He didn't move for a long second, and after that he shook his head.

Count to five before you jump off the damn cliff, Fay had told him; and remember the damn parachute.

He laughed.

"One," he said, and ran for the stairs.

The hell with the parachute; this was more fun.